STUDIES IN ENGLISH PHILOLOGY

STUDIES IN ENGLISH PHILOLOGY

Edited by
MASAHIKO KANNO
and
KAZUKO MATSUURA

KEISUISHA

Hiroshima, Japan

2006

©Masahiko Kanno 2006

Printed in August 2006

Publishied by

Keisuisha Co., Ltd

1-4 Komachi, Naka-ku, Hiroshima 730-0041

JAPAN

ISBN4-87440-940-7 C3082

Acknowledgements

We take this opportunity to thank all of the colleagues of English philology for their contributions to this collection of essays.

Finally, special thanks go to President Itsushi Kimura and all the staff of Keisuisha Publishing Co., Hiroshima, for publishing this volume.

Masahiko Kanno
Kazuko Matsuura

Contents

Acknowledgements

Nicholas Grimald the Humanist Archaist
　　　　　　　　　　　　　　　Masahiko Agari ······ 5

Sidney's Animification and Personification in *Certain Sonnets*:
　　In Comparison with Those in Spenser's *Amoretti*
　　　　　　　　　　　　　　　Kazuko Matsuura ······ 21

Notes on Salinger's Word-formation
　　　　　　　　　　　　　　　Motoko Sando ······ 37

Character Sketch by Metaphor in *Oliver Twist*
　　　　　　　　　　　　　　　Saoko Tomita ······ 55

"Black" and "White" in *Jane Eyre*
　　　　　　　　　　　　　　　Koichi Totani ······ 73

"Kinde" and Related Terms in John Gower's *Confessio Amantis*
　　　　　　　　　　　　　　　Masahiko Kanno ······ 87

Contributors ································· 139

3

Nicholas Grimald the Humanist Archaist

Masahiko Agari

Archaism is related in two ways, Erasmus says, to the unusual style intended by Classical rhetoric to have attracted the audience's or reader's attention: to use archaic words "taken from writings abandoned by posterity on account of their age", and obsolete words "that have vanished completely into disuse", both of which he says should be used "only rarely" (Erasmus 21-2). Together with this Classical influence, the vernacularism of early 16th-century England urged the poets like those in Tottel's *Songes and Sonettes* (1557) to explore old poets, particularly Chaucer, for the authoritative poetic resources. Thus archaism was for them one of the important technical problems. The present paper concentrates on Nicholas Grimald (?1520-?1562), now little known but "the chief representative of humanism" in the *Songes* (Berdan 350), to see how the new Humanist poet tried to write new poetry by making such an exploration and how he was succeeded by Spenser a generation later.

Earlier 16th-century poets looked also for the linguistic treasures kept pure in northern dialects because many old Middle English words had become "restricted to Scots or northern dialects" after 1500 (Görlach 139). The year 1500 may be set as watershed in which old things and words change to new. Hence arose Anglo-Saxonism, whether genuine or pretended. It is taken for granted that in principle there should be no obsolete words in the prose quotations from 1500-1557 in the OED, because the contemporary prose writers in general aimed at using clear English so that there would be no hindrance to clear and easy understanding on the part of the reader. It would be unthinkable that there is an archaism which is used also in an ordinary, serious prose writing. A rare case could happen, though, when for instance legal and poetic archaisms could coincide, but it would be rare indeed.[1]

Then we can find three kinds of archaism in the *Songes*:
1. Poetic archaisms: when the OED quotes from poetry (p) even after 1500.
2. Obsolete words revived: when there is no quotation in 1500-1557.
3. Dialectal archaisms: northern dialects, even in 1557.

And as Grimald's particular case we can find a fourth kind:
4. Pseudo-Anglo-Saxonisms: imitations of OE word-formation.

Next, to make our observation more exact, we will screen the examples thus collected (words, word-meanings, forms), by using contemporary prose writings printed in 1500-1557 as representing the common serious discourse. For instance *to amoue*, i.e. "move inwardly", can be taken to be archaic in the OED quotations (1374Chaucer-1497-1513Douglas-1596Spenser), but we may conclude it is not, because the word is used by Elyot (1531). As the works suitable for such prose-screening we will choose the following prose works (though more should be consulted for the better observation):

Thomas Elyot (c.1490-1546), *The Boke named The Governour* (1531).

John Cheke (1514-57), *The hurt of sedicion* (1549).

Thomas Wilson (1524-81), *The rule of Reason* (1551).

──, *The Arte of Rhetorique* (1553).

By this double process the following list may be given as the archaisms of Nicholas Grimald in his poems printed in the first edition of Tottel's *Songes and Sonettes* (1557). (*Numerals after a word denote a poem's number and a line as given in Rollins's edition. **Abbreviations: (p)=poetry Cax=Caxton Ch=Chaucer D=Douglas Dun=Dunbar H=Henryson Sh=Shakespeare Sk=Skelton Sp=Spenser *SC*=*Shepheardes Calender* ***Numbering in **bold** means the example cited in the OED ****Symbol -|- : A vertical line shows the word in question appearing between the preceding and succeeding dates.)

1. Poetic archaisms

1. *balefull* 165. 92 deadly, destructive 1000...1400*DestrTroy*(p)-|-1592Sh...1862. (Not in Ch, but in Sp and *SC* Ja 27; Jul 23; Oct 29; Nov 145; Dec 149) "Until recent times almost exclusively poetic" (OED).

2. *beurn* 165. 54 a berne, i.e. warrior, hero *Beow*...1515*ScotishFeilde* (p)-1528Lyndesay*Dreme*(p). (Not in Ch or Sp) "...after 1400 the word was retained chiefly in the north, where it was a favourite term of alliterative poetry; in the form *berne* it survived in Scotch till after 1550" (OED).

3. *bewedded* 155. 15 to wed 1000-1205-1513D*Aen*(p). (Not in Ch

or Sp)

4. *blee* 132. 8 colour (of the face) 1225...1500-**1557**-1615-1700-1834. (Not in Ch or Sp) As seen in "colour 888...1460-1623-1850", the word is of OE origin, "A purely poetical word in ME, which gradually became obs. in the course of the 16th or early in the 17th c. (not in Shakespeare)" (OED).

5. *depaynt* 140.29   1325-1374Ch...1450-1509Hawes(p)-|-1598. (In Ch and Sp, *SC* Apr 69 *depeincten*)

6. *freke* 156. 13 a warrior, man   *Beow*...1555(p)-|-1605. (Not in Ch or Sp) "*poet. Obs.*" (OED).

7. *gayn* 165. 40 against   1200...14..-1529Sk(p). (Not in Ch or Sp) "Not known in OE" (OED).

8. *goom* 150. 17 a gome, i.e. man   *Beow*-1205...1450-1515(p). (Not in Ch or Sp)

9. *leaches* 155. 3 a leech, i.e. physician   900...1386Ch...1513D*Aen*(p)-|-1590Sp...1870. (In Ch and Sp, not in *SC*) The word *physician* is first used in 1225.

10. *leef* 154. 14 lief, i.e. agreeable   *Beow*...1387-1541Wyatt(p)-|-1575-1590Sp...1844. (In Ch and Sp, *SC* Jul 165)

11. *naamkouth* 137. 14 namecouth, i.e. known by name   1000...1514D*Aen*(p)-**1557**. (Not in Ch or Sp) Characteristic of OE word-formation.

12. *ofspring* 166. 52 the offspring 949...1460-1547Surrey*Aen*(p)-|-1577...1881. (Not in Ch but in Sp. Not in *SC*)

13. *prest* 140. 13 readily   1297...1475Sc(p)-1547Surrey*Aen*(p)-|-1557-8(p). (Not in Ch. In Sp, not in *SC*)

14. *renkes* 133. 16 a rink, i.e. man, warrior   *Beow*...1515*Scottish Field*(p)-1535Stewart*CronScot*(p)-**1557**. (Not in Ch or Sp) "Only

poet." (OED). See also Grimald 165. 95.

15. *reyled* 165. 87 to rail, i.e. flow, gush   1400-1440-1513D*Aen*(p)-|-1591Sp-1600. (Not in Ch. In Sp but not in *SC*)

16. *ryfe* 143. 2 rife, i.e. speedily, readily   1338...1450-1525(p). (Not in Ch. Not in Sp or *SC* in this sense)

17. *seg* 165. 98 a segge, i.e. man   *Beow*...1508D-15..*ScotishFeilde*-1557-1567-1567. (Not in Ch or Sp) "In the 16th c. only *contemptuous*" (OED), but not so in Grimald, who applies the word to Zoroas the Egyptian astronomer.

18. *shend* 166. 8 to bring to destruction   900...1500(p)-1549-62(p)-|-1600(p)...1906. (In Ch, Sp "to injure", *SC* "to disgrace")

19. *sire* 166. 18 a lord, master   1297...1513D*Aen*(p)-|-1586Sydney...1812. (In Ch, Sp and *SC*)

20. *soote* 2. 1 sweet   1225...1374Ch-1385Ch...1503(p)-|-1558(p). (In Ch, not in Sp who uses *sweet*. In *SC adv.* uses (twice) of *soote*, o.w. *sweet*) See Surrey 2. 1.

21. *stern* 165. 97 brave, severe, cruel   1000...1386Ch-1475-1547 Surrey*Aen*(p)-|-1607Sh...1859. (In Ch, Sp, *SC*) In the 16th century the word seems to have been a poetic archaism, used by Dunbar and Surrey and followed by Grimald and Spenser. Exceptionally, Wyatt in the *Songes* does not use it.

22. *vere* 128. 3 spring   1325...1374Ch...1513D-1529Sk(p)-|-1563. (In Ch, not in Sp) See Surrey 5. 19; 11. 4.

23. *woon* 129. 40 to won, wone, i.e. dwell, live   *Beow*...1513D*Aen*(p)-|-1558Phaer*Ene*(p)...1667Milton...1867. (In Ch and Sp, *SC* Feb 184)

24. Use of a *pa.pple* prefix *y-*: (In Ch, Sp, *SC*)

   yblest 140. 25   1297...1422-|-1591.

   ycleaped 162. 21 called   950...1513D*Aen*-|-1581...1900.

ycutt 165. 20

Note: The following is an ambiguous case: *wight* 148. 7 a man 1200...1386Ch...1500-20Dunbar-1550-|-1567-1579*SC* Apr 47...1869. (In Ch, Sp and *SC*) See Surrey 5. 15; Wyatt 104. 8, to both of whom the word seems to have been an archaism. But, as the word is used in Robert Crowley's pamphlet in 1550, it can be regarded as belonging in the common stock of vocabulary (though it is not certain whether Grimald has adopted it as a poetic archaism from Wyatt and Surrey or as a word already having passed into the common vocabulary).

2. Obsolete words revived

1. *agilted* 129. 44 to aguilt (*a* intensive), i.e. to be guilty towards 1175...1386Ch-1420. (In Ch, not in Sp) The *intransitive* use appears in 1000...1420. The only *causative* use of "to make guilty" appears in 1530 Palsgrave *Lesclarcissement* (from the part of English-French dictionary).
2. *aknow* 166. 29 to come to know, recognize 933-1330-1430. (Not in Ch or Sp) "Very rare after OE. period exc. in pa.pple" (OED). Chaucer's use is *ben aknowe* "be conscious". Thomas Wilson also uses the form *be acknowen* (f. 57) prevailing in the 16th century: see the quotations in the OED.
3. *areard* 162. 84 to arear, i.e. erect 800...1494-|-1571-1627. (Not in Ch. In Sp *FQ* III.12.30)
4. *bebledd* 165. 10 to bebleed, i.e. cover with blood 1230...1485Cax-|-1600...1866. (In Ch. Strangely not in Sp)
5. *beknow* 158. 3 to acknowledge, confess 1325...1386Ch-1440-|-1580. (In Ch. Not in Sp)

6. *bewrap* 160. 38 to clothe 1225...1491Cax-|-1578-1609. (Not in Ch or Sp)
7. *bones* 138. 5 the body 1398...1489Cax-|-1563-87-1601Sh...1953. (In Ch and Sp. Not in *SC*)
8. *chieftanes* 165. 93 a military leader 1330-1400-|-1568...1847. (Not in Ch. In Sp, not in *SC*)
9. *dearworth* 162. 62 dearly esteemed, beloved 1225...1422-**1557**. (In Ch "precious". Not in Sp or *SC*) The sense "precious" appears in 888...1374Ch...1422.
10. *fate* 163. 34 death 1430Lydg-|-1635...1852. (Not in Ch. In Sp but not in *SC*)
11. *fone* 165. 103 foes 14-17 centuries (In Ch and Sp, not in *SC*) Cf. Spenser *foen*, "an archaism" (Sugden, § 16).
12. *girded* 165. 21 to strike, cut, pierce 1205...1460-|-1606...1618. (In Ch, not in Sp in this sense)
13. *kyndly* 138. 6 natural, innate 971...1480Cax-|-1587-1590Sp-1607 Sh. (In Ch and Sp. Not in *SC*)
14. *kouth* 141. 2 couth, i.e. noted, renowned 1000...1400-**1557**. (In Ch. Not in Sp)
15. *molde* 155. 12 garden-soil 1340-1420-|-1601...1828. (Prob. not in Ch or Sp)
16. *olds* 129. 17 wold, i.e. forest 786...1400-50. (Not in Ch or Sp)
17. *ouerwhelms* 155. 16 to cover 1450-|-1573-80...1878. (Not in Ch or Sp)
18. *payzd* 150. 18 to peise, i.e. weigh 1430Lydg-**1557**-1559. (Not in Ch. In Sp but not in *SC*)
19. *place*, in 133. 16 immediately 1290...1425-|-1600...1675. (Not in Ch. In Sp but not in *SC*)

20. *Present* 166. 35 instantly   1381Ch-1386Ch-|-1595-1654. (In Ch and Sp. Not in *SC*)
21. *quaile* 129. 8 to decline, fail   1440-1460-|-1568-1579Sp...1880. (Not in Ch. In Sp and *SC* Nov 91)
22. *rayd* 149. 3 to array   1387...1470-|-1600-1600. (Not in Ch. In Sp but not in *SC*)
23. *retreat* 160. 30 to retrete, i.e. treat of again, reconsider   13.-1374 Ch. (In Ch, not in Sp) OF *retreter*, L *retractare*.
24. *sacred* 162. 93 consecrated, hallowed   1412-20Lydg-|-1590Sp-1611Sh...1885. (Not in Ch. In Sp)
25. *sance* 137. 3 sans, i.e. without (*sance pere* peerless)   1320...1471 Cax-|-1587-1588Sh-1600Sh...1979. (In Ch and Sp. Not in *SC*)
26. *sawes* 165. 83 a decree, command   1300...1440-|-1566-1595Sp. (Not in Ch. In Sp but not in *SC*)
27. sophie 165. 67 wisdom, knowledge   1440-**1557**-1588. (Not in Ch or Sp)
28. *stalworth* 154. 22 strongly built   1175...1494-|-1565...1890. (Not in Ch or Sp)
29. *staunch* 154. 22 that which stops   1400-50-**1557**-1567...1790. (Not in Ch or Sp; verb in Ch and Sp, but not in *SC*)
30. *stounds* 160. 47 a hard time   1000...1374Ch-|-1590Sp. (In Ch and Sp. In *SC* "a sharp pain") Cf. Grimald *stownd* 140. 6 position **1557**-1566-1567-1567-1570-15.. . Though this word seems to have been a poetic archaism in the 16th century, used in the sense "a short time" by Skelton, Spenser (*SC, FQ*) and in "a sharp pain" by Dunbar, Rolland (1550), Spenser (*SC* and *FQ*, where other meanings are exploited, "time, stroke, assault, sorrow"); yet it is used in the sense "a short time" also in the prose of a schoolbook,

William Horman's *Vulgaria* (1519) (English-Latin sentences for schools). In this last, etymological meaning at least, therefore, the word cannot be esteemed to be archaic.

31. *Sythe* 135. 9 thereupon 950...1512. (In Ch. Not in Sp in this sense)
32. *thews* 139. 15 a virtue, good quality 1205...1400-|-1575. (In Ch but not in Sp) Grimald uses the word also in 159. 6; 161. 9. The etymological meaning of this word of OE origin is "usage, custom".
33. *vttrest* 142. 2 utterest, i.e. most outward 1200...1374Ch...1491. (In Ch. Not in Sp) The form *utter* "outward" is common in the 16th century.

3. Dialectal archaisms

1. *-and* 165. 23 as *shinand*, i.e. shining (In Ch, Sp and *SC*) A northern dialectal form of OE and early ME *-ende*; unfamiliar to E.K. who glosses *glitterand* as *glittering* (Jul 177). In the second and subsequent editions the word is changed to *shining*.
2. *anger* 165. 91 physical pain 1377Langl-1500-|-1659-1698. (Prob. not in Ch or Sp) "Still *dial*." (OED). EDD: "inflammation" (north.).
3. *beak* 152. 3 to beek, i.e. expose to the warmth of sun, fire 1230... 1400-1553...1774. (Prob. not in Ch or Sp) Cf. "Now only *Sc.* or *north.dial.*" (OED). EDD: "To bask in the sun or warmth of a fire" (Sc. etc.).
4. *brats* 131. 12 a child 1505Dun-1557-**1577**...1879. (Not in Ch or Sp) Also in Grimald 151. 8. He may have taken it from Dunbar. EDD: "A child, gen. used as a term of contempt or disparagement" (Sc. etc.).

5. *fere* 154. 36 a companion   975...1420-1535*ChroSc*-|-1572...1880. (In Ch and Sp, not in *SC*) See also 160. 21. Grimald may have taken it as poetic archaism from Surrey 15. 46, who first (1547) used it in the sense "mate". EDD: "A friend, companion" (Sc. etc.).

6. *greeted* 157. 7 to weep, cry   *Beow*-725...1549*-|-**1557**-1579Sp...1893. (In Ch: "Northern dial."- Robinson. Prob. not in Sp but in *SC* Apr 1) "Now only *Sc.* and *north. dial.*" (OED). EDD: "To cry, weep" (Sc. etc.).

Note 1549*: *Complaint of Scotland* is a collection of Scottish songs.

7. *stowrs* 166. 15 stour, i.e. a cloud of spray   1513D*Aen*-|-1822. (In Ch "battle", Sp and *SC* "conflict, tumult") "*Sc. Obs. rare*" (OED). EDD: "battle, conflict, tumult" (dialectal use in Sc. etc.).

8. *vnthirld* 143. 11 unsubjugated   1533-1536. (Not in Ch or Sp) "*Sc.Obs.*" (OED). The two quotations are in Scots. The verb *to thirl* is of OE origin. EDD: "To pierce, thrill, shudder" (Sc. etc.).

9. *whiles* 139. 8 sometimes   1480H(p)-1550(p)-|-**1557**-1661...1886. (Prob. not in Ch or Sp) The first two quotations are in Scots. EDD: "Sometimes" (dialectal use in Sc. etc.).

4. Pseudo-Anglo-Saxonisms

1. *afterfall* 161. 6   later happening (Rollins). Not in the OED. Probably Grimald's coinage after OE word-formation.

2. *ayelife* 129. 8 eternal life. Not in the OED. Probably Grimald's coinage.

3. *begynns* 165. 38 (the four) elements. Not in the OED in this sense; citing 1596Sp in the sense "beginning". Grimald uses the old verb as a descriptive noun.

4. *dartthirling* 162. 70 dart-piercing, i.e. piercing with a dart (*to thirl* "pierce" 1000...: see (3) 8 above). Not in the OED.
5. *fingerfeat* 141. 8 lit. finger art. Not in the OED.
6. *forereading* 162. 37 foreseeing. Cited as the only example in the OED.
7. *heauensman* 166. 45. Not in the OED.
8. *hertpersyng* 166. 80 1590Sp "his hart-percing dart"-1647...1870. (Not in Ch but in Sp)
9. *peeplepesterd* 129. 15 overcrowded with people. The only example in the OED.
10. *Swanfeeder* 162. 54 the Thames. Not in the OED.

Note: The compound *gaynstriue* (166. 47 to strive against, oppose 1549-62(p)-**1557**-1590Sp [Not in Ch. In Sp]) is composed of two words of OE origin, but as this pretended Anglo-Saxonism itself is not old or unprecedented, it is not admitted here as archaism.

Total occurrences: (1) 24 (2) 33 (3) 9 (4) 10 **Total 76**

These results will be observed closely.

(1) Grimald and Chaucer

(1) **Poetic archaisms**. Of the total 24 poetic archaisms, 10 (42%) are used also by Chaucer.

(2) **Obsolete words revived**. Of the total 33, 16 (48%) are used also by Chaucer.

(3) **Dialectal archaisms**. Of the total 9, 4 (44%) are used also by Chaucer (his *stour* is counted).

(4) **Pseudo-Anglo-Saxonisms**. Of the total 10, none is used by Chaucer. 7 are not mentioned in the OED. It seems that these 10 words are of Grimald's coinage.

It is concluded, first, that in the first three sections the words Grimald and Chaucer have in common amount to 30 (45%) of his total uses (66); then, that Grimald relies on Chaucer for dialects to nearly the same degree, and last, that Grimald's Pseudo-Anglo-Saxonism is outstanding; he needed no Chaucer, no Surrey or Wyatt or other poets, only his own sense of pure Anglo-Saxonism.

His historical Anglo-Saxonisms may be observed in *blee, freke, naamkouth, aknow, arear, old, beurn, renk, seg, vnthirld*.

(2) Grimald and other materials

In Section (1), there are (near-)contemporary transmitters of Chaucer to Grimald: Stephen Hawes (*depaynt*), Gavin Douglas (*leaches, sire, vere, woon, y*-prefix), Wyatt (*leef*), and Surrey (*soote, stern, vere*). On the other hand, there are direct predecessor-poets on whom Grimald seems to rely for the archaisms without Chaucer as model: Douglas (*bewed* fr.OE, *naamkouth* fr.OE, *reyled*), Surrey (*offspring* fr.OE, *prest*). Douglas and then Surrey are conspicuous in either case.

In Section (2), the words of OE origin that Chaucer does not use are only 3: *aknow, areard*, and *olds*, where part of Grimald's Anglo-Saxonism may be found.

In Section (3), the dialect words and form that both Chaucer and Grimald use are -*and, fere, greeted*, and *stowrs* (though in the last the two poets' meanings are different from each other). It will be natural that these words are of OE origin except two of unknown origin (*beak* and *brats*) and one of AF, OF (*stowrs*).

In Section (4), Grimald seems to have created the compounds

(*begynns* excepted) in the mould of OE word-formation. It is possible that he was influenced by Sir John Cheke who acted as the leader of Cambridge Humanists (Berdan 356), when he studied there (BA 1540). The compound *forepointed* (144. 5 to appoint beforehand) may be mentioned here as indicating a probable influence on Grimald of Cheke who adopted OE word-formation in his English translation of Matthew.

(3) **Grimald and Spenser**

In Section (1), of the total 24 archaisms, 8 (33%) are used in *The Shepheardes Calender* (1579): *baleful, depaynt, leef, sire, stern, woon, y*-prefix; *shend* "injure" included. In other works of Spenser, 12 (50%) are found: *baleful, depaynt, leaches, leef, offspring, prest, reyled, shend, sire, stern, woon, y*-prefix. Grimald's poetic archaisms have found their way to Spenser in total 12 words. But one word seems to have been rejected: *soote* is used only twice and adverbially (*SC*), otherwise *sweet* is substituted both in the *SC* and in the *FQ* and other works. The form *soote* (adj.) seems to have ceased around 1600 (see OED).

In Section (2), of the total 33 words, only 2 (6%) are found in the *SC*: *quaile* and *stounds* (though the second is different in meaning). In other works of Spenser into which the above 2 have entered, as many as 15 (45%) are found: *areard, bones, chieftanes, fate, fone, kindly, payzd, in place, present, quaile, rayd, sacred, sance, sawes,* and *stounds*.

In comparison, Grimald's poetic archaisms in (1) are slightly more long-lived and viable in frequency than his obsolete words revived.

In Section (3), of the total 9, 3 (33%) are used in the *SC*:

17

suffix *-and, greeted,* and *stowrs* (different in meaning). In other works of Spenser, 3 are used, *stowrs* included: suffix *-and, fere,* and *stowrs.* His total uses amount to 4 (44%).

In Section (4), only *hertpersyng* lives long, first adopted by Spenser after Grimald.

To sum up: of Grimald's total 76 archaisms, 32 (42%) are found in Spenser, and 30 (39%) in Chaucer. Grimald is but slightly inferior to Spenser in resorting to the *well of English undefiled.*

(4) Chaucer, Grimald, and Spenser

(1) The archaisms used all by Chaucer, through Grimald's senior poets, Grimald, and Spenser amount to 8 (33%): *depaynt, leaches, leef, shend, sire, stern, woon,* and *y*-prefix.

(2) Chaucer's words, revived by Grimald and received by Spenser, amount to 6 (18%): *bones, fones, kindly, present, sance,* and *stounds.*

(3) Chaucer's words and form, also used by Grimald's senior authors, Grimald, and Spenser are 4 (44%): *-and, fere, greeted,* and *stowrs, -and* being already a northern dialect form in Chaucer's time.

(4) Chaucer has no relation to Grimald's pretended Anglo-Saxonism.

What archaisms are found in common in the three poets are 18 (27%) of the total 66 (the last section excluded). Of the three kinds of archaism (18), the poetic archaism (8) is comparatively the most continuative (44%; followed by 33% and 22%).

(5) Problems of Early Modern English archaism

The more exact prose-screening would be effectuated by examining more prose works published in 1500-1557, but in reality a problem seems still to remain: could archaisms not be used in prose, as Erasmus says they are to be used "only rarely"? Indeed, E.K. in 1579 glosses and defends using *couthe* in the *SC* Jan., saying it is used also in prose by Thomas Smith and Gabriel Harvey. About a generation before, in the 1540s and early 50s when Grimald was engaged in composing, the Humanistic movement in favour of poetic archaism had been enhanced by the printing particularly of Chaucer's works in 1532. Then in 1553 Thomas Wilson did complain among others that "The fine Courtier wil talke nothyng but Chaucer" (*Rhet.* f. 86v). A courtier writer could easily use Chaucerisms even in prose as well as in poetry, because he thought he could be well understood among the courtly circle. The verb *to clepe* (129. 10), used also by both Chaucer and Spenser (not in the *SC*) and listed by Speght, had already been used in the 1523 *Act 14 & 15 Hen. VIII* "called and cleaped", probably as a common word (or a legal term?). Or *atween* (150.16), noted by the OED as "the usual form in north. dial., but only a poetic archaism in the literary language", occurs once in Thomas Wilson (1551).[2] According to our standard of observation both are not archaisms. But the problem is that it is difficult to decide whether these old and dialectal words had already got into the common stock of vocabulary or they were merely used as archaisms by the writers. The latter supposition, however, may deny the very idea of archaism, and at the preliminary stage of our trial observation the former will be a practical way to promote this difficult subject of archaism.

Notes

1 Some leading articles on Early Modern English archaism start or conclude their discussions on the basis that archaisms can be found also in other discourses like prose. See for instance McElderry, Osselton, Adamson.
2 Other discarded examples are *amoue* (165.69) / *eke* (165.66) / *spill* (150.11 "destroy") / *a cold* (162.76) / *eloquence* (163.39) / *forgo* (165.102 "go away") / *forgone* (160.19 "part with") / *hore* (166.65 "hoar") / *leasure* (143.9 "deliberation") / *lothesom* (166.51) / *pase* (162.39 "step") / *preserud* (166.32 "keep from perishing") / *saw* (162.8 "story") / *skylfull* (165.75 "full of knowledge") / *to* (166.32 "too, extremely").

Text

Songes and Sonettes (1557) (Menston: Scolar Press, 1973).

Works cited

Adamson, Sylvia, "Literary Language," in *The Cambridge History of the English Language*, Vol. III 1476-1776, ed. Roger Lass (CUP, 1999), 577-9.
Berdan, J. M., *Early Tudor Poetry 1485-1547* (NY: Macmillan, 1920, 1951).
Erasmus, Desiderius, *On Copia of Words and Ideas*, tr. D. B. King & H. D. Rix (Milwaukee: Marquette U P, 1999).
Görlach, Manfred, *Introduction to Early Modern English* (CUP, 1993).
McElderry, B. R. Jr., "Archaism and Innovation in Spenser's Poetic Diction," *PMLA* XLVII (1932), 144-70.
Osselton, Noel, "Archaism," in *The Spenser Encyclopedia*, gen.ed. A. C. Hamilton (Toronto: U of Toronto P, 1990), 52.
Rollins, H. E. ed., *Tottel's Miscellany*, 2 vols. (Cambridge: Harvard UP, rev. ed. 1966).
Speght, Thomas, "The old and obscure words in Chaucer explained" in *The Workes of ...Geffrey Chaucer* (1598, 1602), ed. D. S. Brewer (Menston: Scolar Press, 1969).
Sugden, H. W., *The Grammar of Spenser's Faerie Queene* (NY: Kraus Reprint, 1966).
OED 2nd edition on CO-Rom version 3.0.
EDD: *The English Dialect Dictionary*, 6 vols., ed. Joseph Wright.

Sidney's Animification and Personification in *Certain Sonnets*: In Comparison with Those in Spenser's *Amoretti*

Kazuko Matsuura

1. Introduction

Personification is the trope that has been extensively used not only in the poetic language but also in our ordinary language. Wales (2001: 294) defines this as "a figure of speech or trope in which an INANIMATE object, ANIMATE non-human, or ABSTRACT quality is given human attributes". Similarly, Ricoeur (2003: 68) states that it turns an inanimate, non-sentient, abstract, or ideal entity into a living being and feeling, into a person and reminds us of "the metaphorical transfer from the inanimate to the animate" as the family of metaphor.

The Renaissance era was when many writers used a great variety of rhetorical devices. Bloomfield (1963: 163) argues that "The period from 1200 to 1700 was the great era of personification allegory in European literature". We can tell this trope, that is, personification, as he puts it, is one of the most typical Renaissance devices contemporary poets preferably employed in the sixteenth century. It is, of course, true of Sir Philip Sidney (1554-86) and Edmund Spenser (1552?-1599). In addition, Sidney himself admires it for "that high flying libertie of conceit proper to the Poet" in *The Defence of Poesie* (1581: 6-7), citing David's Psalms which he calls a heavenly poesy in which personification like "his telling of the beasts joyfulnesse, and hils leaping" is involved. Therefore, this paper aims to highlight how these two Renaissance poets personify or animize something into another in terms of a leading character, namely, a man's feeling toward the woman he loves and compare those characteristics. The works used are *Certain Sonnets* (1581) written by Sidney and *Amoretti* (1595) written by Spenser.

2. Animification and Personification

There have been a considerable number of studies made on personification. As for Sidney's personification, it is important to note that, as Hedley (1982: 67) points out, Sidney's handling of personification is an a-temporal, a-topical order in his *Astrophil and Stella*. From a grammatical point of view, Bloomfield (1963: 163-165) considers personification a violation of grammatical rule and we can find it by some grammatical tests, such as the use of nouns as names of living beings or gods, verbs which are usually only used of living thing, the use of vocative. Besides, it can be done by dropping the definite article of the animated noun, what he calls "deictification", from the grammatical point of view. He, however, discusses we should focus on the predicate. The point is personification is the combination of the non-metaphoric subject and metaphoric predicate and then it connects the concrete and the metaphoric at the same time. This is a useful clue to judge whether some expression is a true personification or not. From a cognitive point of view, Kövecses (2002: 49-50) observes that taking time for example, we view it as the thing that is completely independent from human beings, and thus it can be seen as an agent, like a thief, reaper and so on. This thought comes from George Lakoff and Mark Turner (1980: 5) and, to put it simply, we can understand any metaphor through our daily experience. Goatly (1997: 48-49) developed their conceptualization and structured the metaphorical lexicon by certain analogies. He divides metaphors into five categories, which are General Reifying, Specific Reifying, Personifying Abstract and Animizing, Materializing Abstract Process, Process=Process and Object= Object. Here, in particular, we would like to deal with only the category of such Personifying Abstract and Animizing as Idea/Emotion=Human or Abstract Animal. Moreover, Paxon (1994: 42-43) classifies personification into seven major categories from the standpoint of ontology: substantialization, anthropomorphism, personification, animification, reification which is related to ideation and topification. What I would like to pay attention here in particular are personification and animification. In other words, there are six subcategories by which he classifies ontological domains: human, non-human life form (plant or animal), inanimate object, place, abstract idea, deity. Therefore, the method I would like to employ is Goatly's Root Analogies mentioned above and Paxson's taxonomy since it is of great use to make clear his feeling by analyzing how each word is transferred into another word by personification or animification and thus we could add some more categories to his Root Analogies. Here we would like to deal with only personified or animized man's feelings. We divided each item according to *Bunruigoihyou* which tells us the order of each word. Let us now examine each animification and personification and then take a close look at each poet's characteristics.

3. Spenser's Animification and Personification
3.1. Animification
3.1.1. Human=Animal: Fowls/Bird

> (1) Lyke as *a byrd* that in ones hand doth
> desired food, to it doth make his flight:
> euen so my hart, that wont on your fayre eye
> to feed his fill, *flyes* back vnto your sight. (73)

We have two examples out of 7 in which the man who cannot control his feeling thinks so much of her that he sees himself as a bird. Thus, this is the case where his heart is compared to a bird. He often praises her eye's beauty through the sonnets. This kind of expression, 'fly to someone', is still familiar to us in modern time when excited. In the previous sonnet, his mind is also animized as a bird.

3.1.2. Human=Animal: Myriapod/Spider

> (2) I Ioy to see how in your drawen work,
> Your selfe vnto the Bee ye doe compare;
> And me vnto *the Spyder* that doth lurke,
> In close awayt to catch her vnaware. (71)

Here he is compared to a spider while she is a bee. The bee, mentioned as, she who got stuck in a spider's web is about to be eaten by a spider. De Vries states a spider's web strikes us as a labyrinth of love. Therefore, this leads me to the idea that he as well as she got stuck in a labyrinth of love.

3.1.3. Human=Animal: Mammal/Deer

(3) Lackyng my loue I go from place to place,
   lyke *a young fawne* that late hath lost the hynd:
   and seeke each where, where last I sawe her face,
   whose ymage yet I carry fresh in mynd. (78)

After this sonnet, the man feels deeply depressed because he will get married soon and cannot see her. His wondering feeling of love is reflected in this word by a simile. According to De Vries, a fawn represents timidity and it suggests his cowardness toward her.

3.1.4. Human=Animal: Mammal/Horse

(4) Then as *a steed* refreshed after toyle,
   out of my prison I will break anew: (80)

We have a similar example where he appears as if a horse tired from love. De Vries observes that a horse is a symbol of lust in Renaissance and he seems to try to restrain his feeling.

3.2. Personification
3.2.1. Mind: Mind/Emotion=Human

(5) VNquiet thought, whom at the first I *bred*,
   Of th'inward bale of my loue pined hart:

25

and sithens haue with sighes and sorrowes *fed*,
till greater then my wombe thou woxen art. (2)

Here it is clear that his effusive love including pleasure and sorrow is revealed. We notice his love is borne in his heart and steadily growing. Among his personification, this is the most dynamic and energetic example in which his feeling of love is expressed like a human.

3.2.2. Mind: Mind/Emotion=Human

(6) Her breast that table was so richly spredd,
My thoughts *the guests*, which would thereon haue fedd. (77)

In this sonnet, the table is richly spread with dishes and this is compared to her body. Besides, there are two apples on it and they imply her breast. He regards his feelings as the guests who welled up naturally. Expressing his emotion as an invited guest makes him livelier. The effect is immeasurable. If it were a human, that is, himself, I would not have such a deep impact.

3.2.3. Mind: Mind/Emotion=Human

(7) but ioy her thrall for euer to remayne,
And yield for pledge my poore *captyued* hart; (42)

This describes that his heart is taken away from her beauty and he is falling love with her. It is the typical instance used even in the modern time.

4. Sidney's Animification and Personification
4.1. Animification
4.1.1. Body: Eyes=Animal: Mammal/Mole
    Human=Animal: Insect/Fly

> (8) Mine eyes thence drawne, where lived all their light,
>   Blinded forthwith in darke dispaire did lye,
>   Like to *the Mowlle* with want of guiding sight,
>   Deepe plunged in earth, deprived of the skie.
>   ···Even as the flye, which to the flame doth goe,
>   Pleased with the light, that his small corse doth burne:
>   Faire choice I have, either to live or die
>   *A blinded Mowlle*, or else *a burned flye*. (21)

He decides to leave her since the more he sees her eyes, the more he likes her. He deeply regrets his decision as soon as he left her. Then he finds himself in a miserable situation in which he likens himself to a mole and a fly at the same time. He encounters a tough choice between a life without her, or a blind mole, and a painful love with her, or a burned fly.

4.1.2. Human=Animal: Fish/Fish

> (9) *A stranger fish*, my selfe not yet expired,
>   Though rapt with beautie's hooke, I did impart
>   My selfe unto th' Anatomy desirde,
>   In stead of gall, leaving to her my hart:
>   Yet live with thoughts closed up, till that she will
>   By conquest's right in steade of searching kill. (22)

In this sonnet, the Seven Wonders of the United Kingdom is shown in odd numbers and the man's feeling in even numbers. This is the very example of an a-topical order of what Hedley remarks. For example, in the previous paragraph, he mentions a fish which stays still alive, even though its gall is taken away. In this connection, he is a fish while she is a hook. Furthermore, he offers her his heart and he is of course still alive. In short, his thought for her is so persistent.

4.2. Personification
4.2.1. Mind: Nature/Reason=Human
      Mind: Sense/Sense=Human

(10) With violence of heav'nly
    Beautie tied to virtue,
    Reason abasht retyred,
    Gladly *my senses* yeelded,
    Gladly *my senses* yeelding,
    Thus to betray my hart's fort,
    Left me devoid of all life; (25)

This stanza is made up of personified 'Senses'. Here he admits that 'Senses' finally won 'Reason', though 'Senses' used to conflict with 'Reason'. It is worth noting that paradox is used in the fourth and fifth lines.[1] To yield is, of course, not a pleasing deed, but using this paradox creates a certain kind of unique effect, which is mixed feelings between joy of love and sorrow in losing his reason. As a result, this leads to next personified 'Desire'.

4.2.2. Mind: Desire/Desire=Human

> (11) SLEEPE *Babie* mine, Desire, nurse beautie singeth:
> Thy cries, ô *Babie*, set mine head on aking:
> The *Babe* cries 'way, thy love doth keepe me waking'
> ···Since babie mine, from me thy watching springeth,
> Sleepe then a litle, pap content is making:
> The *babe* cries 'nay, for that abide I waking'. (6)

This stanza is conspicuous for personification of 'Desire'. The baby, namely 'Desire', would continue to cry, talking to him because of your love. While he is in love with her, the baby never stops crying unless he gains 'pap', or her love. The fact that he personifies desire as a 'baby' means his decision to grow desire. I would like to note that 'Desire' is also depicted as a family member here. There is a strong connection between love and desire, as the saying that there is no parent but loves their children goes.

4.2.3. Life: Hurt/Pain=Human

> (12) THOU *paine the onely guest of loath'd constraint,*
> *The child of curse, man's weaknesse foster-child,*
> *Brother to woe, and father of complaint*: (10)

He explains four sonnets in a row from the sonnet (8) consisting personification of pain were written when she had some pain in her face. Here he personifies pain not only as a physical one, but also as a mental one. In the first line, he describes it as irremovable thing easily and in the following lines, we find out his pain is dear as well as serious in terms of calling it a member of the family.

4.2.4. Matter: Fire/Fire, Air/Air, Sea/Sea=Human

> Heaven and earth: Earth/Earth=Human
> Language: Rumor/Fame=Human[2]
> Time: Time/Time=Human
> Place: Place/Place=Human

> (13) *THE fire* to see my wrongs for anger burneth:
> *The aire* in raine for my affliction weepeth:
> *The sea* to ebbe for griefe his flowing turneth:
> *The earth* with pitie dull the center keepeth:
> *Fame* is with wonder blazed:
> *Time* runnes away for sorrow:
> *Place* standeth still amazed
> To see my night evils, which hath no morrow. (3)

This stanza provides a fine example of personification, using verbs toward the nouns which cannot usually be personified. The whole nature revolves around him. In other words, everything surrounding him seems to sympathize with his despairing feelings. This kind of personification is repeated one more time in the latter of the same stanza in which he asks every nature to kill him. He ardently hopes that every nature is on his side. In the end, however, he feels his death would be in vain since he is not loved by her.

4.2.5. Heaven and earth: Earth/Earth=Human

Body: Head, eyes, nose and face/Eyes
(14) *That heavie earth*, not fierie sprites may plaine?
  That eyes weepe worse then hart in bloodie teares?

Here we have two kinds of personification in which he personifies the earth and eyes. The former shows that he made the earth complain about her who treats him coldly. In short, the adjective 'heavy' and the verb 'complain' suggest his troubles. The latter explains we see how deep his sorrow is by making his eyes weep purposely.

5. A data comparison of Spenser and Sidney

This section will deal with how things are animized and personified in each writer's sonnets. Let us show you the following tables:

Table 1 The Frequency of Animification and Personification

	Animification	Personification	Total
Spenser	7	4	11
Sidney	5	103	108

First of all Spenser's *Amorettie* is composed of 89 sonnets while Sidney's *Certain Sonnets* is 32. Thus, Spenser's number of sonnets is approximately three times as many as that of Sidney. Taking it into consideration, we see from Table 1 that Sidney's ratio of animification and personification is much higher than that of

Spenser. Besides, with regard to personification, Sidney uses it approximately 25 times more than that of Spenser despite the number of sonnets. One of the causes of this is due to a great deal of repetitions he uses. Let us now turn to what kind of things two writers use in animification and personification.

Table 2 Spenser's Animification

	Animification		
Mammal	3	Reptile	1
Fowl	2	Myriapod	1

Table 3 Spenser's Personification

	Personification
Mind	4

Concerning Spenser's animification, Table 2 shows that half of it is mammals, which is extremely near to human. As a consequence, it gives us such an impression that we easily link him with some kind of animal. Furthermore, animized 'fowl' is really a typical one. We notice that he animizes 'reptile' or 'myriapod' in particular when he would like to present his impulse of love. Likewise, he often animizes 'mammal' when he feels depressed. On the other hand, he animizes 'fowl' when he is content with his love. As for personification, we find just one kind, which is the 'mind'.

Table 4 Sidney's Animification

	Animification		
Fowl	2	Insect	1
Fish	1	Mammal	1

Table 5 Sidney's Personification

	Personification		
Mind	48	Language	3
Life	21	Place	3
Matter	10	Time	3
Heaven and earth	9	Heavenly body	2
Body	3	River	1

In the case of Sidney, there are more animals other than mammals compared to Spenser. What we have in common with Spenser is 'fowl'. Regarding his personification, there are as many as 10 kinds where we notice he indeed personifies various things, such as nature, natural phenomenon, or even ourselves. Above all, half of them are related to 'mind' which is used to represent his sorrowful situation because of her cold attitude. Besides, 'life', which ranks secondly on the table, is employed for showing his heart's pain.

6. Final Remarks

So far we have compared how Spenser and Sidney use animification and personification. From the viewpoint of Sidney, the number of his personification is outstanding despite the fact that his number of sonnets is much smaller than Spenser. It follows from this that in Sidney's sonnets, personification plays a vital role to describe how miserable his situation is, receiving severe attitudes from the woman he loves. The tables shown earlier clarify his uniqueness, using everything surrounding him, while Spenser comparatively employs traditional ones. His uniqueness is also reflected in (9) incorporating many legends into his personification. Throughout this analysis, it is concluded that the way of Sidney's personification is more vivid than that of Spenser.

Notes

* I would like to express my appreciation to Dr. William Shang at Kibi International University for reading the manuscript and improving my English. Any inadequacy, however, is all mine.
1 Leech (1969:132) mentions paradox is an absurd statement, while oxymoron is "yoking together of two expressions which are semantically absurd".
2 OED, s.v. fame, n^1. 1.a.

Texts

Osgood, C. G. & H.G. Lotspeich, eds. (1966, 1947) *The Works of Edmund Spenser, The Minor Poems,* A Variorum Edition Vol.8, Part Two. Baltimore: The Johns Hopkins Press.

Ringler, W. A. Jr. ed. (1962) *The Poems of Sir Philip Sidney.* Oxford: Clarendon Press.

References

Bloomfield, M.W. (1963) "A Grammatical Approach to Personification Allegory." *Modern Philology.* 60: 161-71.

de Vries, Ad. and Arthur de Vries. (2004) *Elsevier's Dictionary of Symbols and Imagery.* 2nd, enlarged ed. Amsterdam: Elsevier.

Feuillerat, A. ed. (1968) *The Prose Works of Sir Phillip Sidney.* Vol. III. Cambridge University Press: Cambridge.
Goatly, A. (1997) *The Language of Metaphors.* London and New York: Routledge.
Hedley, J. (1982) "What Price Energeia: Personification in the Poetry of Sidney and Greville." *Studies in the Literary Imagination.* 15 (1): 49-66.
Kövecses, Z. (2002) *Metaphor A Practical Introduction.* Oxford University Press: Oxford.
Lakoff, G. and M. Turner. (1980) *Metaphors We Live By.* Chicago: University of Chicago Press.
Leech, G. N. (1969) *A Linguistic Guide to English Poetry.* London: Longman.
Paxon, J.J. (1994) *The Poetics of personification.* Cambridge University Press: Cambridge.
Ricoeur, P. (2003) *The Rule of Metaphor.* Trans. Robert Czerny. London and New York: Routledge Classics.
Simpson, J. and E.S.C. Weiner, eds. (2004) *The Oxford English dictionary.* 2nd ed. CD-ROM, Version 3.1. Oxford University Press: Oxford.
The National Institute for Japanese Language Publications ed. (2004) Bunruigoihyou. Tokyo: Dainippontosho.
Wales, K. (2001) *A Dictionary of Stylistics.* 2nd ed. London: Longman.

Notes on Salinger's Word-formation*

Motoko Sando

0. Introduction

In present-day English, particularly in American English, new words, phrases or expressions are frequently produced through changes in the culture and ideas, and there are several ways which lead to these neologisms.

Salinger makes his novels more distinctive and idiosyncratic by combining various parts of speech, often utilizing hyphens to fashion new words, using affixes, and sometimes changing word classes. His practice of coinage, however, seems to be slightly different from one story to the next.

So far, a number of studies on *The Catcher in the Rye* have been made from not only literary but also linguistic points of view; Costello (1959), Ando (1968), Konishi (1981). Namba (1984: 38-9) points out that Salinger chose to characterize the hero Holden through his preference of new compound adjectives; these compounds are coined from familiar nouns/adjectives by simply adding *-ed*, *-y* or *-looking*. Kobayashi (1977) also deals with Salinger's word-forming practice found in *Nine Stories*. However, *Franny and Zooey* and *Raise High the Roof Beam, Carpenters and Seymour: an Introduction* have somehow been neglected, although in fact they abound in compounds.

The present paper aims to examine and classify Salinger's word making practices in *The Catcher in the Rye, Nine Stories, Franny and Zooey* and *Raise High the Roof Beam, Carpenters and Seymour: an Introduction.*

1. Compounds

Compounding is the easiest way to make new words because it simply combines more than two existing lexical items. Compounds can be written either as complete single words, phrases, or they can be hyphenated; the most popular type in Salinger's works is the hyphenated variety in which distinct lexical items are freely united together.

1.1. Adjectival Compounds

In Salinger's stories, adjectival compounds are the most frequent, and they may be divided into the following six types.

1.1.1. Adjective + *-looking* type

The adjective plus *-looking* form is used in thirteen stories, except *Uncle Wiggily in Connecticut.* This type is a predominant feature in Salinger's works:

Table 1

Catcher	awful-looking [75], beat-up-looking [211], cheap-looking [196], corny-looking [14], Cuban-looking [90], distinguished-looking [61], dumpy-looking [90], flitty-looking [85], funny/funnier-looking [85], good-looking [85, 106, 124], inexpensive-looking [108], mossy-looking [22], scraggy-looking [197], terrific-looking [85], weak-looking [170]

Notes on Salinger's Word-formation

Bananafish	ordinary-looking [16]
Eskimos	funniest-looking [43], good-looking [44]
Laughing	condemned-looking [56]
Dinghy	good-lookin' [76]
Pretty	distinguished-looking [116]
Blue	odd-looking [146], unendowed-looking [139], underprivileged-looking [144]
Esmé	chronographic-looking [99-100], efficient-looking [91], messy-looking [103], military-looking [93]
Teddy	debilitated-looking [166], good-looking [174], new-looking [166-7]
Franny	anonymous-looking [22], right-looking [11, 20]
Zooey	anonymous-looking [122], citational-looking [120], dampish-looking [50], endless-looking [50], gorgeous-looking [176], imperial-looking [88], mobile-looking [129], occultish-looking [73], organic-looking [187], Persian-looking [142], soiled-looking [188], stubby-looking [114], sunburned-looking [201], used-looking [75]
Carpenters	bullish-looking [30], daunted-looking [20], formidable-looking [14, 32], good-looking [72], oppressive-looking [11], resolute-looking [55], terrific-looking [8], unintrepid-looking [52]
Seymour	developed-looking [182], innocent-looking [117] pullable-looking [165], unsalutary-looking [103]

(Each title is given here in abbreviated form. Full title with year of publication is given in the appended list of Texts.)

It seems that Salinger uses this type of word compounding in order to emphasize Holden's awareness of the phoniness of people around him in *The Catcher in the Rye*:

39

(1) At this other tiny table, right to my left, practically on *top* of me, there was this <u>funny-looking</u> guy and this <u>funny-looking</u> girl. They were around my age, or maybe just a little older...but she was even <u>funnier-looking</u> than *he* was, so I guess she *had* to listen...On my right there was this very Joe Yale-looking guy, in a gray flannel suit and one of those <u>flitty-looking</u> Tattersall vests...Anyway, this Joe Yale-looking guy had a <u>terrific-looking</u> girl with him. Boy, she was <u>good-looking</u>. But you should've heard the conversation they were having. [*Catcher*, 85]

(Page number is shown in the square bracket immediately after each quotation. Italics are original and underlines text my emphasis.)

This type of compounding is also used to qualify non-human objects: *condemned-looking bus* [*Laughing*, 56], *unendowed-looking three-story building* [*Blue*, 39], and *innocent-looking Blake lyric* [*Seymour*, 117].

1.1.2. Noun/Verb + *-y* + *-looking* type

All examples in Table 2 are taken from *The Catcher in the Rye*. *Pimpy-looking* and *show-offy-looking* are Holden's favorite expressions, and they are also used without *-looking*, as will be seen in 2.1.1.:

Table 2

Catcher	bleedy-looking [3], hoodlumy-looking [81], pimpy-looking [69], show-offy-looking [69], vomity-looking [76, 80], whory-looking [69, 80]

40

Notes on Salinger's Word-formation

It is to be noticed that *vomity-looking* is only used for modifying an inanimate noun:

(2) Anyway, that's what I was thinking about while I sat in that vomity-looking chair in the lobby. [*Catcher*, 80]

1.1.3. Noun + *-ing* participle type

Some adjective compounds are made up of an object noun and ...*-ing*:

Table 3

Catcher	ice-skating [128]
Esme	house-counting [92]
Blue	bill-filling [157]
Teddy	cross-bearing [176]
Franny	forehead-bumping [8]
Zooey	bunny-loving [172], eyebrow-raising [88], joy-making [69], knee-cramping [180], world-hating [148]
Carpenters	congregation-dispersing [14]
Seymour	breast/forehead-smiting [130], Chekhov-baiting [212], hand-rubbing [142], marble-shooting [208, 209], poetry-loving [114], stairs-bounding [189]

Bill-filling, derived from "fill the bill," is used in the sense of "perfectly suitable" or "apt:"

(3) I'm tempted to say that Thursday evening was peculiar, or perhaps macabre, but fact is, I have no bill-filling adjectives for Thursday evening. [*Blue*, 157]

41

Cross-bearing, derived from "bear one's cross," is used as an adjective to modify *grimace* in the following:

(4) She shut her eyes and waited, with a <u>cross-bearing</u> grimace, till Myron moved. [*Teddy*, 176]

1.1.4. Noun + Adjective or Adjective + Noun type

Table 4

Eskimos	bed-dishevelled [43]
Dinghy	stern-end [80]
Esmé	automatic-arrest [105]
Blue	self-trained [147], self-detached [149], special-delivery [135], summer-active [165]
Teddy	Jesus-brilliant [168]
Franny	super-male [5], burly-set [6]
Zooey	frosted-glass [91, 110], glass-paned [122], mirror-faced [75], mottled-gray [129]
Carpenters	clear-Havana [17, 46], hip-pressed [17], late-afternoon [16], morocco-bound [44]
Seymour	funny-lookingness [180], multiple-vitamin [172], near-doctorine [207], needle-sharp [130], super-gossamer [177]

The next is uttered by a husband who got angry at his wife's words:

(5) "That's a <u>Jesus-brilliant</u> thing to say," Mr.McArdle said quietly-steadily, addressing the back of his wife's head. [*Teddy*, 168]

42

1.1.5. Adjective + Adjective type

Table 5

Esmé	soaking-wet [93]
Blue	high-breasted [135], super-chic [135]
Zooey	bogus-courageous [142], deadly-bookish/deadly-cute [53], macabre-comic [156], quasi-consructive [71], semi-easy [180], solid-sounding [182], static-dynamic [119] super-conservative/super-comforting [142]
Carpenters	deadly-serious [70], little-girlish [33], subnormal-sounding [16]
Seymour	advantage-disadvantage [169], Semitic-Celtic [122], snaky-hipped [197], spanking-new [122], sub-acoustical [135], unfelicitous-sounding [107]

Static-dynamic and *macabre-comic* consist of two words with opposite meanings coordinated. *Deadly* or *super* as the first adjective serves to intensify the second adjective, meaning "very" or "ultra" respectively; in (6), *deadly-bookish* and *deadly-cute* characterize *questions* as being "very formal and very affected:"

(6) ...all seven of the children had managed to answer over the air a prodigious number of alternately deadly-bookish and deadly-cute questions... [*Zooey*, 53]

(7) At least he wears horrible neckties and funny padded suits in the middle of that frightened, super-conservative, super-comforting madhouse. [*Zooey*, 141-2]

1.1.6. Hyphenated Compounds over three words

When writers cannot express a situation they want to describe with existing words, they have often recourse to a kind of impromptu expression. In the popular media, such hyphenated compounds are frequently overused to attract people's attention. This is regarded as "nonce word" (Wales, 2001[2]: 272), "group compound" (Ootsuka & Nakajima, 1987: 236), or "some kind of block language" (Konishi, 1981: 343-4).

A variety of words of this type, generally consisting of three or four words, are found in Salinger's stories, except *The Catcher in the Rye*:

Table 6

Laughing	almost-All-America [57], side-of-the-mouth [62], some-girls-just-don't-know-when-to-go-home [64]
Uncle	forty-seven-room [23], hut-hope-hoop-hoop [35]
Esmé	don't-tell-me-where-to-put-my-feet [109]
Blue	after-*you*-Alphonse [133], below-shoulder-length [147], brushed-and-combed [142], goose-in-flight [145], live-and-let-live [133], next-to-the-last [152]
Zooey	brick-and-concrete [180], eight-inch-thick [181], faculty-recreation-room [65], meant-to-be-picked-up [180], one-foot-up [151], one-two-three [91], permanently-left-behind [180], pre-notification-of-death [73], second-time-over [101, 102], twenty-one-inch-screen [119], uncertain-what-to-do-with [180]
Carpenters	come-back-soon [62], oil-and-vinegar [67], tried-and-true [77], what-have-you [27, 65], you-know-how-men-are [34]

Seymour	curiously-productive-though-ailing [102], footlight-and-three-ring [146], hurry-up-and-get-well-from-your-hepatitis-and-faintheartedness [161-2], knot-to-be [189], movie-*cum*-vaudeville [145], song-and-dance-and-patter [145], twenty-six-inch [205], well-over-the-budget [205], young-widower-and-white-cat [132]

In (8), two students of completely different characters are contrasted:

(8) As roommates, Bobby and I were neither more nor less compatible than would be, say, an exceptionally live-and-let-live Harvard senior, and an exceptionally unpleasant Cambridge newsboy. [*Blue*, 133]

The longest hyphenated compound which is composed of ten words is found in *Seymour: an Introduction*:

(9) At this moment, I'm wearing that handsome firmament he offered me as a hurry-up-and-get-well-from-your-hepatitis-and-faintheartedness present down around my knees. [*Seymour*, 161-2]

In the following citation describing the interior of a room, there are lots of books disorderly scattered, beside a sofa and a table. The word *book* is used six times here:

(10) The rest, with very little exaggeration, was books. Meant-to-be-picked-up books. Permanently-left-behind books. Uncertain-what-to-do-with books. But books, books. [*Zooey*, 180]

1.2. Noun Compounds

Although not as common as adjectival compounds, noun plus noun patterns are also found in several short stories. It is interesting to note that most of the noun compounds in Table 7 are used to describe people:

Table 7

Pretty	celebrity-genius [120]
Esmé	truth-lover [92], statistics-lover [92]
Blue	agent-appraiser [131], leper-kisser [163], realist-abstractionalist [157]
Teddy	ankle-sneakers [167], apple-eaters [191, 196] quietness-steadiness [167] <cf. quietly-steadily [168]>
Franny	outburst-inburst [22], tearer-downers [17], word-squeezers [13]
Zooey	Buddha-truth [105], Christ-Consciousness [172], dream-interpreter [127], player-characters [49], privacy-lover [91], Tolstoy-lovers [61], Vermont-marble [124]
Carpenters	actress-singer [41], fellow-passengers [64]
Seymour	artist-seer [105], fellow-artists [114], fellow-raconteurs [142], God-hater [113], God-knower [106], God-lover [113], income-supplementers [115], music-lover [155(twice)],

46

| Seymour | poetry-lovers [117], shot-caller [170], stallion-laugh [194], Zen-killers [97] |

In (11), *quietness-steadiness* refers to a "quiet and calm way of speaking:"

(11) When it was on vacation from its professional chores, it fell, as a rule, alternately in love with sheer volume and a theatrical brand of quietness-steadiness. [*Teddy*, 167]

In this connection, the adverbial compound *quietly-steadily* appears on the next page of the story:

(12) "That's a Jesus-brilliant thing to say," Mr.McArdle said quietly-steadily, addressing the back of his wife's head. [*Teddy*, 168]

Outburst-inburst consists of two opposite terms coordinated to describe the character's emotional change:

(13) And yet, when finally she stopped, she merely stopped, without the painful, knifelike intakes of breath that usually follow a violent outburst-inburst. [*Franny*, 22]

2. Derivation

The formation of new lexical items by adding affixes to existing words is called "derivation" and as popular and productive as compounding. Derivation generally changes the word classes; in

Salinger's writings, derivational suffixes are preferred. Sando (2003: 62-3) mentions that noun plus *-y* form, noun/adjective plus *kind of* form and noun/adjective plus *type* form are found in *The Catcher in the Rye*. We will see this word-forming pattern in more detail.

2.1. Adjectives derived by suffixation
2.1.1. Noun/ Verb + *-y* type
In colloquial usage, it is quite common for nouns/verbs to be turned into adjectives through the addition of *-y*, meaning "somewhat like:"

Table 8

Catcher	burny [195], Christmasy [197], faggy [2], perverty [201], pimpy [101], show-offy [84], vomity [81], whory [69], wheeny-whiney [94]
Esmé	watty [104]
Teddy	lipsticky [175]
Zooey	campusy [139], hair-shirty [161], test-tubey [139]

Wheeny-whiney may be considered to be reduplicative. Interestingly, *The Oxford English Dictionary* (2002^2, hereafter abbreviated as *OED*^{2}) cites *The Catcher in the Rye* as the earliest instance of *vomity*. *OED*^{2} gives the following quotation, and defines the word as "redolent of vomit:"

> (14) The cab I had was a real old one that smelled like someone'd just tossed his cookies in it. I always get those vomity kind of cabs if I go anywhere late at night. [*Catcher*, 81]

In (15), the spectators of two football teams are compared by means of two coordinated pairs of adjectives, *deep and terrific* and *scrawny and faggy; faggy*, derived from the verb *fag*, means "sparse:"

(15) You couldn't see the grandstand too hot, but you could hear them all yelling, deep and terrific on the Pencey side, because practically the whole school expect me was there, and scrawny and faggy on the Saxton Hall side, because the visiting team hardly ever brought many people with them. [*Catcher*, 2]

2.1.2. Noun/Adjective + *-like* type

Derivatives using the suffix *-like* as well as *-in* or *-wise* are widespread in contemporary English. According to Biber *et al* (1999: 553), the suffix *-like* is especially versatile in its capacity to create new adjectives from nouns. Both hyphenated and non-hyphenated types are attested as follows:

Table 9

Bananafish	winglike [10]
Laughing	amateur-like [64]
Teddy	reedlike [167]
Franny	knifelike [22]
Zooey	almanaclike [54], alisthenic-like [172], Buddy-like [189], connoisseurlike [81], coterielike [54], dossier-like [51], trophylike [120], voidlike [22], X-ray-like [82]
Carpenters	bottleneck-like [14], cadetlike [15], multi-flashbulb-like [13],

| Seymour | bayonetlike [29], Heinzlike [108], obituary-like [106], *trompe*-like [177] |

2.1.3. Noun/Adjective + *-type* type

In formal English, the word *type* is normally followed by the preposition *of*, whereas in colloquial English this word can frequently do without the preposition. The suffix *-type* can be added to nouns and adjectives, and non-hyphenated forms are also used. Exceptionally, *Bible-type* in *The Catcher in the Rye* modifies an inanimate noun *book*:

Table 10

Catcher	Bible-type [110], impatient-type [82], screwed-up type [117]
Esmé	letter-writing types [88]
Blue	Continental-type [131], Peter Abelard-type [158]
Zooey	deep-type [63], pilgrim-type [158]
Seymour	deep-type [194], earnest-type [172], eleven-point type [124], physical-type [212], self-employed type [144], vivid-type [170]

3. Conversion

"Conversion" or functional shift, is a word-formation technique whereby one word class switches to another without any change in form. Wales (2001[2]: 85) observes that nouns commonly become verbs; also verbs and adjectives are turned into nouns:

(16) She's quite skinny, like me, but nice skinny. Roller-skate

skinny. I watched her once from the window when she was crossing over Fifth Avenue to go to the park, and that's what she is, <u>roller-skate</u> skinny. [*Catcher*, 67]

As Namba (1977: 36) points out, *roller-skate* is "a noun used as an adverb of degree (intensive word)." The repeated use of *skinny* is impressive, particularly strengthened by the use of *roller-skate*, which suggests the sport the girl is good at.

Two nouns, *Dixieland* and *whorehouse* in (17), are linked together as an adverbial modifier descriptive of a certain singer's record:

(17) She sings it very <u>Dixieland and whorehouse</u>, and it doesn't sound at all mushy. [*Catcher*, 115]

(18) and (19) are quoted from *Teddy*, both of which are spoken by the same person; nouns are used as nonce-verbs here:

(18) "I'll <u>exquisite day</u> you, buddy, if you don't get down off that bag this minute. And I mean it," Mr. McArdle said. [*Teddy*, 166]

(19) "I'll <u>Queen Mary</u> you, buddy, if you don't get off that bag this minute," his father said. [*Teddy*, 169]

Mr. McArdle's son Teddy makes the following statement a few moments earlier: "We passed the Queen Mary at three-thirty-two this morning, going other way, if anybody's interested." Mr.

51

McArdle is upset because his son often sits down on his favorite bag, despite warnings not to do so. This is a kind of "echo utterance," in which Mr. McArdle expresses his indifference to the object of his son's interest. This short story begins with (18), but we may safely assume that *exquisite day* also serves as an echo expression.

4. Final Remarks

The present paper has dealt with Salinger's word-forming devices under three main classes of compounds, derivatives and converted forms. We also have observed how he took advantage of them finding that adjectival compound is the most popular type in his writings.

It is said that the Salinger's writing style becomes more religious after *The Catcher in the Rye*, and that there is an increase in the length of the stories published after *The Catcher in the Rye*, beginning with *De Daumier-Smith's Blue Period*.

The Catcher in the Rye, written in the first person, is full of colloquial expressions and slang, while it is rich in repetitions and metaphors. However, it is rather short of those kinds of word formation that we have been discussing above. Although *Uncle Wiggily in Connecticut* and *The Laughing Man*, for instance, are quite short not amounting to one-tenth the length of *The Catcher in the Rye*, they both owe their vitality to Salinger's language, which is partly sustained by his innovative word formations.

Thus Salinger's word-forming method effectively functions in that it gives his writing style effective means to prevent it from being monotonous, and he seems to be successful in holding readers' attention lest they should get bored. Most of the characters in Salinger's stories are young, usually teenagers or people in their twenties. Salinger seems to make abundant use of compounds or derivatives, partly to make up for their poverty of expression and partly to suggest their immaturity.

---

* This article is a revised version of a paper read at the 32nd meeting of the Japan Society of English Usage and Style, held at Kansai University on June 21, 2003. I would like to thank Dr. Kevin Collins at Wakayama University, who kindly corrected my stylistic errors. All remaining inadequacies and inconsistencies are, of course, my own.

Texts

Salinger, Jerome David. 1951. *The Catcher in the Rye*. [*Catcher*] Boston: Little, Brown and Company. (Paperback edition, 1991)

Salinger, Jerome David. 1953. *Nine Stories*. Boston: Little, Brown and Company. (Paperback edition, 1991)
   (1948) 1. *A Perfect Day for Bananafish* [*Bananafish*]
         2. *Uncle Wiggily in Connecticut* [*Uncle*]
         3. *Just Before the War with the Eskimos* [*Eskimos*]
   (1949) 4. *The Laughing Man* [*Laughing*]
         5. *Down at the Dinghy* [*Dinghy*]
   (1950) 6. *For Esmé – with Love and Squalor* [*Esmé*]
   (1951) 7. *Pretty Mouth and Green My Eyes* [*Pretty*]
   (1953) 8. *De Daumier-Smith's Blue Period* [*Blue*]   9. *Teddy* [*Teddy*]

Salinger, Jerome David. 1961. *Franny and Zooey*. Boston: Little, Brown and Company. (Paperback edition, 1991)
   (1955) *Franny* [*Franny*]   (1957) *Zooey* [*Zooey*]

Salinger, Jerome David. 1963. *Raise High the Roof Beam, Carpenters and Seymour: an Introduction*. Boston: Little, Brown and Company. (Paperback edition, 1991)
   (1955) *Raise High the Roof Beam, Carpenters* [*Carpenters*]
   (1959) *Seymour: an Introduction* [*Seymour*]

References

Ando, Sadao. 1968. "*The Catcher in the Rye* no Eigo (6)." *Gendai Eigo-Kyōiku* 6, 40-41.
Biber, Douglas, et al. 1999. *Longman Grammar of Spoken and Written English*. London: Longman.
Costello, Donald P. 1959. "The Language of *The Catcher in the Rye*." *American Speech* XXXIV: 3, 172-181.
Kobayashi, Yoshitada. 1977. "Salinger no Eigo no Zōgo-teki Hyōgen – *Nine Stories* wo Chushin ni – ." *Eigo-Seinen* 3, 24.
Konishi, Tomoshichi. 1981. *America-Eigo no Gohō*. (*Aspects of American English*.) Tokyo: Kenkyusha.
Namba, Tatsuo. 1977. "J. D. Salinger no *The Catcher in the Rye* ni mirareru Meishi oyobi Daimeishi kara Tenyō sareta Fukushi matawa Fukushi-Sōtōku." *Miyazaki-Ikadaigaku Kiyo* 2:1, 25-38.
---. 1984. *The Language of Salinger's 'The Catcher in the Rye.'* Tokyo: Shinozaki Shorin.
Ootsuka, Takanobu and Fumio Nakajima eds. 1987. *Shin-Eigogaku Jiten*. (*Dictionary of English Linguistics and Philology*.) Tokyo: Kenkyusha.
Quirk, Randolph, et al. 1985. *A Comprehensive Grammar of the English Language*. London: Longman.
Sando, Motoko. 2003. "Some Aspects of Salinger's Vernacular Language in *The Catcher in the Rye*." *ERA* 20, 53-71.
Simpson, J. A. and E. S. C. Weiner, eds. 2002. *The Oxford English Dictionary*. 2nd edition on CD-ROM, Version 3.0. including Additions Series Volumes 1-3. New York: Oxford University Press.
Wales, Katie. 2001. *A Dictionary of Stylistics*. 2nd edition. London: Longman.

Character Sketch by Metaphor in *Oliver Twist*

Saoko Tomita

1. Introduction

Dickens's novels mostly make use of rhetorical representations with which characters, their thoughts and ideas, or even objects surrounding them are vividly or symbolically displayed. Brook (1970: 30) remarks on the frequency and effectiveness of Dickens's metaphors and similes in his literary works since these devices full of elaborate and imaginative depictions give the reader an opportunity to not only imagine the appearance or behaviour of the characters vividly in their own mind but also receive a certain impression of it. In *Oliver Twist*, we can see a great frequency in the use of metaphor and simile, with 210 and 219 examples of each respectively. Because of the considerable figures, both devices are of great use in the depiction of the theme of the novel, that is, the miserable life of Oliver Twist an innocent orphan who experiences his social life surrounded by the good or evil world. The metaphoric expressions, however, not only indicate comical or humorous aspects of the story, but also suggest profound meanings of the inimical world of the adults who surround Oliver. Dickens often uses metaphor to depict characters as if they were animals or lifeless objects, but it is characteristic of his style that the majority of his metaphors are rich in humour, imagination and accuracy of observation. In other words, he employs metaphor as a medium for implying each character's inner thoughts or emotions towards other characters evoked from his or her life, experience, and even the society which deeply influences him or her. This paper, therefore, aims first to highlight the linguistic features of Dickens's metaphor in terms of their forms and techniques, and second, to make a detailed analysis of character so that we can better understand Dickens's rhetorical aims in the novel.

2. Devices of Metaphor

The use of metaphor goes back to the period of Chaucer and the device has been frequently employed by various poets like Spencer, Shakespeare or Wordsworth as a means for rhetoric or embellishment in English literary works. According to Brooke-Rose (1958: 23-24), metaphor is "any replacement of one word by another, or any identification of one thing, concept or person with any other." It is worthy of remark to find how this replacement or identification can be made through words in Dickens's novels. I shall use her explanation of metaphor and her analysis of metaphorical structures as a framework for analysing the characteristics of Dickens's technical devices in *Oliver Twist* from a syntactic point of view.

2.1. Noun Metaphor

According to Brooke-Rose's classification, the patterns of noun metaphor are basically categorised into five types, namely: (1) *Simple Replacement*, (2) *The Pointing Formulae*, (3) *The Copula*, (4) *The Link* With "*To Make*" and (5) *The Genitive*.[1] Brooke-Rose deals with the metaphorical syntax of different English poets from different periods (e.g. Chaucer, Spencer, Shakespeare, Blake, Keats, and Wordsworth) and makes a close observation of the emblematic meanings inside their metaphors, which can be identified and construed by the readers from the context. Although her analysis is mostly focused on poems, it is possible to apply her types to Dickens's metaphors, since most of his descriptions consist of nouns or noun phrases, e.g. "the hue of her [Rose Maylie's] countenance had changed to *a marble whiteness*" (257; ch.XXXIII). In this context, the expression "a marble whiteness" represents Rose's physically ill condition as well as her natural pureness.

The following examples show the most typical types of noun metaphor employed by Dickens in *Oliver Twist*:

Type 1: (Det.) + N.
(1) The angry flush had not disappeared, however; and when he was pulled out of *his prison*, he scowled boldly on Noah, and ... (51)
(2) "Must go before the magistrate now, sir," replied the man. "His worship will be disengaged in half a minute. Now, *young gallows*." (76)

Type 2: (Det.) + Adj. + N.
(3) "What? What?" interposed Mr. Bumble: with a gleam of pleasure in *his metallic eyes*. (48)

Type 3: N. + Copula + Adj./N.
(4) I wish some well-fed philosopher, *whose meat and drink turn to gall within him; whose blood is ice, whose heart is*

iron; could have seen Oliver Twist clutching at the dainty viands that the dog had neglected. (31)

Type 4: The Verb *Make* + N.^{1} + N.^{2}

(5) ... although, within such walls, *enough fantastic tricks are daily played to make the angels blind with weeping*, they are closed to the public, save through the medium of the daily press. (81)

Type 5: N.^{1} + of + N.^{2}

(6) The air became more sharp and piercing, as its first dull hue: *the death of night, rather than the birth of day*: glimmered faintly in the sky. (219)

To start with, the first type, (*Det.*) + *N.* as in (1), is the most frequent pattern of all as it includes 95 examples. Brooke-Rose terms this type of metaphor *Simple Replacement* and explains the linguistic phenomenon as follows:

> The proper term of the Simple Replacement metaphor is not mentioned and so must be guessed: we either have to know the code or the code must be broken. [...] My point is that Simple Replacement is on the whole restricted to the banal, the over-familiar, or to metaphors which are so close in meaning to the proper term that the guessing is hardly conscious; or that they depend much more on the general context than do other types of noun metaphors. (1958: 26)

As mentioned above, the meanings of these types of metaphorical descriptions can be guessed and assumed to be clear from the context or the readers' previous knowledge. Regarding instance (1), Dickens uses the term "his prison" for the dust-cellar into which Oliver was dragged and locked up as punishment after he attacked Noah Claypole violently in Mr. Sowerberry's house. This description is metaphoric in that the locking up of Oliver in the dust-cellar can be associated to his imprisonment as a criminal. Despite Oliver's natural goodness and purity, he is regarded by adults as an evil child, and thus, readers understand the replacement of the proper term *dust-cellar* with the metaphor *prison* from the context. Example (2) also makes a close relationship between Oliver and a prisoner, in this case a prisoner condemned to death, for the vocative phrase *young gallows* symbolically insinuates to the reader that its utterer, Mr. Bumble, shows his indignation or animosity towards Oliver by attacking or expressing contempt for a villainous person like him. In *Oliver Twist*, this noun type is much more frequent than other types, since Dickens is in the habit of characterising human beings as animals or lifeless objects, and by so doing he applies colourful and symbolic meanings to their human qualities.

Next, the form (*Det.*) + *Adj.* + *N.* also performs a rhetorical function in Dickens's metaphor. This form is most effective in symbolising the quality of certain human characters, although we can see no more than 8 examples of this type in the novel. For instance, the expression *his metallic eyes* as in (3) denotes Mr. Bumble's cold-hearted quality because the adjective *metallic* is metaphoric. In other words, the readers are able to infer from the mechanising description - *his metallic eyes* - that Mr. Bumble is not an altogether agreeable person. As Meier (1982: 84) observes,

59

"mechanising human beings as if they were metal or stone almost always points to hard-heartedness, lack of feeling and inflexible rigidity in that particular character," it can be said that Dickens's intention of depicting human characters as objects is not a mere embellishment of description but a symbolisation of their inhuman and life-lacking qualities.[2]

The metaphor type *N. + Copula + Adj./N.* has the second highest frequency in *Oliver Twist* (35 examples). The copula in this case includes a verb such as *be, seem, become, call, turn* and so forth, although in this novel the examples feature the verbs *be, get, turn,* and *pronounce*. The last two types of metaphor classified by Brooke-Rose, namely *The Verb* Make $+ N.^1 + N.^2$ and $N.^1 + of + N.^2$ are very rare in *Oliver Twist*: there is only one example of the former and 11 examples of the latter. Regardless, they are effective forms for Dickens in describing various scenes or the qualities of particular characters colourfully and impressionistically.

2.1.1. Semantic Changes

We have seen some typical types of noun metaphor referring to the examples in *Oliver Twist*. In this section, we will observe their frequencies and make an analysis of the semantic changes between words in order to explicate the mechanics of Dickens's metaphor.

As to Dickens's metaphor, semantic shifts can be divided into four patterns: from *concrete* to *concrete*, from *concrete* to *abstract*, from *abstract* to *concrete*, and from *abstract* to *abstract*. Table 1 indicates the frequency of particular types of semantic shift among the total of 150 noun metaphors. The *concrete* to *concrete* pattern is by far most frequent, with 123 examples in

Table 1 The Frequency of Semantic Shifts on Noun Metaphor

Pattern Type	Concrete ⇒ Concrete	Concrete ⇒ Abstract	Abstract ⇒ Concrete	Abstract ⇒ Abstract
(Det.) + N.	84	2	4	5
(Det.) + Adj.+ N.	7	0	1	0
N.+Copula+ Adj./N.	26	4	3	2
Make + N.¹ + N.²	0	0	0	1
N.¹ + of + N.²	6	3	1	1
Total	123	9	9	9

total. Among these, the most frequent is the *(Det.) + N.* type (84 examples), followed by the *N. + Copula + Adj./N.* type (26 examples).

The following are four patterns of semantic transference which are most frequent in terms of the form *(Det.) + N.*:

A. **Human being > Human being (44 exx.)**

(7) "Then I'll whop yer when I get in," said the voice; "you just see if I don't, that's all, *my work'us brat*!" and having made this obliging promise, the voice began to whistle. (33)

B. **Human being > Artefact (19 exx.)**

(8) "Yer don't know who I am, I suppose, *Work'us*?" said the charity-boy, in continuation: descending from the top of the post, meanwhile, with edifying gravity. (33)

C. **Human being > Supernatural being (6 exx.)**

(9) The Jew again applied his eye to the glass, and turning his ear to the partition, listened attentively: with a subtle and eager look upon his face, that might have appertained

to *some old goblin*. (341)

D. Human being > Animal (5 exx.)

(10) *The dove* (Mr. Bumble) then turned up his coat-collar, and put on his cocked hat; and ... (211)

Example (7) shows Noah Claypole, Mr. Sowerberry's assistant, swearing at Oliver by calling him "a work'us brat" (= a workhouse brat) and thus reducing his human quality to a socially lower level. What is more, Noah's contemptuous behaviour towards Oliver is confirmed by his habit of dehumanising him as "work'us" as in instance (8), for he uses this dehumanisation eleven times in the novel. In fact, Dickens largely uses this type of *dehumanisation* in order to illustrate impersonal or cruel dispositions of particular human characters symbolically and impressionistically. Besides, as to the example (9) the narrator depicts Fagin's devilish appearance regarding him as *an old goblin* by means of metaphor. This description could be understood by readers at first as comical or ludicrous, but undoubtedly the predominant feeling is the fearsome element that predominates in a grotesque image, due to the fact that the dehumanisation in this case takes place not on an imaginative, but on a real level and evokes an association with the fearful world of crime which Fagin lingers around. Although there are only 6 examples of the pattern of shift from *human being* to *supernatural being*, it is very effective in Dickens's technical purpose: he often tends to dehumanise an evil character into a *goblin* or *devil*, which would make a terrifying impact on the reader.

3. Character Sketch

In this section, we will analyse the author's metaphorical descriptions in terms of character sketch and explicate some deep meanings inherent in his use of *dehumanisation*. As Oliver the hero encounters various people from different social classes during the course of the novel, the metaphoric descriptions vary tremendously according to circumstances. We will, therefore, focus on three patterns of semantic changes and display the author's technical effects in the novel.

3.1. Transformation of Human Beings into Artefacts

At the beginning of the novel, Oliver spends his early childhood under unfavourable conditions in a workhouse, where he is at all times treated as a *villain, devil, brute*, or even dehumanised into *an article* or *millstone* especially by Mr. Bumble.

- Oliver > article

    (11) ...and to be guarded from the sins and vices of Oliver Twist: whom the supplication distinctly set forth to be under the exclusive patronage and protection of the powers of wickedness, and *an article direct from the manufactory of the very Devil himself.* (16)

    (12) The next morning, the public were once more informed that Oliver Twist was again *To Let*; and that five pounds would be paid to anybody who would take possession of him. (25)

Although Oliver is naturally pure and good-natured, he is mechanised by the beadle as if he were a lifeless object as in (11).

As Meier (1982: 53) says, "children in Dickens's novels are often pushed around like objects," we can say that the device of dehumanising children into objects or inanimate matter involves an implicit criticism of these characters on the part of the narrator. Similarly, example (12) displays the helpless child treated as a useful object, for the bill to let Oliver was pasted on the gate for the public's information. Fawkner refers to this description and remarks in this way:

> "Behind the grim humour of such witty remarks as "The next morning, the public were once more informed that Oliver Twist was again To Let; and that five pounds would be paid to anybody who would take possession of him," there is bitter indignation at the inhuman exploitation of innocent and vulnerable people like Oliver Twist." (1977: 49-50)

Accordingly, we can see from his view that Dickens not only attempts to humorously depict individual characters as objects, but also attack the typical behaviour of life-denying society and its institutions. Also, Noah's successive descriptions of Oliver as "workhouse" denote the child's low status in the aspect of social class as in (13).

• Oliver > workhouse

(13) "Yer know, *Work'us*," continued Noah, emboldened by Oliver's silence; and speaking in a jeering tone of affected pity: of all tones the most annoying: "Yer know, *Work'us*, it

carn't be helped now; and of course yer couldn't help it then; and I'm very sorry for it; and I'm sure we all are: and pity yer very much. But yer must know, *Work'us*, yer mother was a regular right-down bad'un." (44)

There are 19 examples of this type of *dehumanisation* in the novel. Although Dickens employs this technical device mostly for illustrating Oliver's impersonal or cruel treatment at the hands of others realistically, he tends to portray other people as animals or ghostly figures after Oliver escaped from Mr. Sowerberry's house to London and had an accidental encounter with Fagin the Jew.

3.2. Transformation of Human Beings into Animals

With regard to descriptions that animalise human beings, we can find 15 examples including all the types of noun metaphor mentioned in 2.1. Although animal-metaphor is not so frequent as compared with *human being* to *human being* metaphor, which has 59 examples, it plays a vital role in Dickens's *dehumanisation*.

In later chapters of the novel, Oliver participates in a life of crime and goes into the world of adults around him by virtue of his encounter with Fagin, who orders him to commit a theft with his gang. At first, the Jew is, in Oliver's eyes, so repulsive or grotesque that the child describes him like *a reptile* by means of the simile which follows:

• Fagin > reptile

(14) As he glided stealthily along, creeping beneath the shelter of the walls and doorways, *the hideous old man*

> *seemed like some loathsome reptile*, engendered in the slime and darkness through which he moved: crawling forth, by night, in search of some rich offal for a meal. (147)

This transmutation of the Jew into a *reptile* here represents not only Oliver's fear of the man's ugly appearance itself but also his childish keen observation of the hostile world of delinquency, which he considers dangerous and adverse. In the same way, Oliver animalises the Jew's teeth as if they were *a dog's* or *rat's* as in (15). Meier (1982: 62) observes, "animal metaphors are used with exceeding frequency for the villains in Dickens's novels, and not surprisingly, it is predatory beasts that appear in this context"; we can, therefore, see from the view that he tends to degrade a dislikable human being to an animal-like state so that he can evoke a close analogy between the character and an animal in terms of aggression and ferocity.

- Fagin > dog; rat

(15) His right hand was raised to his lips, and as, absorbed in thought, he bit his long black nails, *he disclosed among his toothless gums a few such fangs as should have been a dog's or rat's*. (378)

- Sikes > hound

(16) "... If you want revenge on those that treat you like a dog — like a dog! worse than his dog, for he humours him sometimes — come to me. I say, come to me. *He is the mere hound of a day*, but you know me, of old, Nance." (362)

On the contrary, Fagin occasionally considers Bill Sikes an animal like *a dog, brute* or *hound*. The term *hound* in example (16) emblematically displays Sikes's brutality and ferociousness as well as Fagin's hatred for him. In *Oliver Twist*, the dehumanising description of a certain character as *a dog* or *beast* is of great importance in that the narrator tends to draw an analogy between the animal and the principal villain of the novel. What is more, Oliver is also regarded as *a two-legged spaniel* by Monks, his half brother, who has despised the hero from his childhood. As he was once brought up in the workhouse and locked up into the dust-cellar as if he were a prisoner in Mr. Sowerberry's house, the dehumanisation of Oliver into *a spaniel* gives the reader an unfavourable impression of him.

In *Olive Twist*, almost all of the implication of an animal-metaphor may be negative, rather than positive, for the novel includes no more than one positive type of *dehumanisation* among the total 15 examples of the device.

3.3. Transformation of Human Beings into Supernatural Beings

In this section, we will focus on the semantic transference from human beings to supernatural beings such as *angel, fairy, god, goddess* and *ghost*. With regard to Dickens's metaphor, this type of dehumanisation is most effective in portraying a villainous and contemptible character as *a devil, monster, goblin, ghost, phantom* or the like, whereas a gracious and sweet-tempered character tends to be described as *an angel, fairy, god* or *goddess*. In *Oliver Twist*, we can see 9 noun metaphors of this device, 7 of which are negative in import.

- Sikes > ghost

(17) Crackit went down to the door, and returned followed by a man with the lower part of his face buried in a handkerchief, and another tied over his head under his hat. He drew them slowly off. Blanched face, sunken eyes, hollow cheeks, beard of three days' growth, wasted flesh, short thick breath; *it was the very ghost of Sikes*. (407)

Excerpt (17) shows the way in which Sikes made his appearance before Toby Crackit, a fellow criminal, after running away from London and lingering around for fear that he would be captured on a charge of murdering Nancy, his mistress, who had tried to help Oliver to escape from the clutches of the gang. However, likening Sikes to his own ghost is rather ironic, for he has suddenly decided to return to London only after finding himself pursued by the ghastly figure of what he thinks is Nancy's corpse; see (18) below. This description by simile implies that he is obsessed with the idea of death as he is haunted by a guilt after the murder.

- Nancy > corpse

(18) Every object before him, substance or shadow, still or moving, took the semblance of some fearful thing; but these fears were nothing compared to the sense that haunted him of that morning's ghastly figure following at his heels. [...] If he ran, it followed — not running too: that would have been a relief: *but like a corpse endowed with the mere machinery of life, and borne on one slow melancholy wind*

that never rose or fell. (388)

3.4. Transformation of Humans into Abstracts

We can also find metaphoric descriptions of a human being regarded as an abstract, although there are only 3 examples in the novel. Although Oliver was often reduced to a less than human quality under the pressure of hostile environments, dramatic changes occurred after he was taken into Mr. Brownlow's house, where all the people treated him with kindness and benevolence. One day when he was sick in bed, he felt calm and happy with Rose Maylie beside him, as the atmosphere of friendliness extends, in his mind, to the environment. As in example (19), abstract words, namely "loveliness and virtue" symbolise Rose's good nature and benevolence, which penetrate into the hero's pure soul.

- Rose > loveliness and virtue

(19) Oliver's pillow was smoothed by gentle hands that night; and *loveliness and virtue watched him as he slept.* He felt calm and happy; and could have died without a murmur. (233)

4. Results and Analysis

Table 2 shows how each character is dehumanised into a non-human living being or inanimate object by means of noun metaphor, and indicates either a negative or positive value of the semantic component from the context.

Table 2 Dehumanisation in Terms of Noun Metaphor

Characters	Words
Oliver (7exx.)	(Artefacts) *article* (−), *receipt* (−), *millstone* (−), *workhouse* (−), *gallows* (−) (Animals) *brute* (−), *spaniel* (−)
Mr. Bumble (3exx.)	(Artefacts) *metal* (−), *waterproof* (−) (Animal) *dove* (+)
Mr. Sowerberry (2exx.)	(Animals) *ice* (−), *iron* (−)
Noah (2exx.)	(Artefacts) *leathers* (−), *charity* (−)
Fagin (6exx.)	(Artefact) *stone* (−) (Animals) *dog* (−), *rat* (−), *cur* (−) (Supernatural Beings) *goblin* (−), *devil* (−)
Bill Sikes (5exx.)	(Animals) *dog* (−), *brute* (−), *brute-beast* (−), *hound* (−) (Supernatural Being) *ghost* (−)
Rose Maylie (7exx.)	(Artefact) *marble whiteness* (−) (Abstracts) *loveliness* (+), *virtue* (+), *comfort* (+), *happiness* (+), *lovely bloom* (+), *spring time* (+)

From the table, it is notable that Dickens makes good use of *dehumanisation* for the purpose of emphasising the inhuman and cruel dispositions of characters who despised or mistreated the miserable orphan. Only Rose Maylie, who treats Oliver kindly, is depicted positively through dehumanising metaphor, and these are abstracts. By so doing, the author not only achieves a comical effect, but also forms his vision of life-denying society and the perverse behaviour of the inimical world which surrounds him.

5. Final Remarks

We have observed the particular patterns of Dickens's metaphor and found that *dehumanisation* is a most effective means of description for implying essential characteristics of various human characters clearly. However, the people in the novel dehumanised into animals or objects tend to be depreciated in the sense of being inhumanly insensitive or cruel so that the author can create an image of the inimical world of crime into which Oliver was drawn.

Notes

1   In *Oliver Twist*, we can see no examples of *The Pointing Formulae*, one of the types suggested by Brooke-Rose, which takes the form of "such or so/such + adj. + N". or "this/that + N". Her detailed account of this type is given in *A Grammar of Metaphor*, 1958, p.68.

2   Dickens's particular method of mechanising a human character into metal is confirmed when we refer to Miss Murdstone in *David Copperfield* whose belongings David associates with her essentially cold and cruel disposition, as he considers her "*a metallic lady*" (p.45, Ch. IV).

Texts

Dickens, Charles. *David Copperfield*. Ed. Nina Burgis. The World's Classics. Oxford: Oxford UP, 1981.

------. *Oliver Twist*. Ed. Kathleen Tillotson. The World's Classics. Oxford: Oxford UP, 1999.

References

Brook, G.L. *The Language of Dickens*. London: André Deutsch, 1970.
Brooke-Rose, Christine. *A Grammar of Metaphor*. London: Secker, 1958.
Collins, Philip. *Dickens and Crime*. 3rd ed. Houndmills, Eng.: Macmillan, 1994.
Fawkner, Harald W. *Animation and Reification in Dickens's Vision of the Life-Denying Society*. Stockholm: Liber Tryck, 1977.

Ginsburg, Michael P. "Truth and Persuasion: The Language of Realism and of Ideology in *Oliver Twist*." *Charles Dickens: Critical Assessments*. Ed. Michael Hollington. 4 vols. East Sussex: Helm Information, 1995. 228-46.

Kincaid, James R. "Laughter and Point of View." *Dickens and the Rhetoric of Laughter*. Oxford: Clarendon, 1971. 162-91.

Meier, Stefanie. *Animation and Mechanization in the Novels of Charles Dickens*. Bern: Francke, 1982.

Miller, D.A. "The Novel and The Police." *Charles Dickens: Critical Assessments*. Ed. Michael Hollington. 4 vols. East Sussex: Helm Information, 1995. 221-27.

Quirk, Randolph. "Charles Dickens, Linguist." *The Linguist and the English Language*. London: Arnold, 1974.

Sugakawa, Eizo. *Eigo Shikisaigo no Imi to Hiyu*. Tokyo: Seibido, 2001. 70-91.

Tomita, Saoko. "Metaphors in *Great Expectations*." *ERA* ns 20.1-2 (2003): 34-52.

"Black" and "White" in *Jane Eyre*

Koichi Totani

When *Jane Eyre* is analysed, it is frequently approached from the viewpoints of feminism and post colonialism. First of all, however, I would like to read author's words faithfully, and so I decide to approach by reading based on traditional grammar. I would like to focus on colour words here and describe what I notice from them. I once picked up all the colour words from *Wuthering Heights* by Charlotte's younger sister Emily and arranged them according to the frequency of occurrence. To take a single instance from the result, and describe briefly Emily's characteristic uses of colour words, I can remark that the word 'black,' which most frequently occurred, was most often used when Emily described one of the characters, Heathcliff, especially his eyes.

According to the book of Mr Seizo Sukagawa, who is engaged in a historical study of English colour terms, 'in Old English, *blæc, hwit, rēad, grēne, ġeolu, purple, græġ* were basic colours, and in Middle English, innumerable borrowings from French flowed into English and it is remarkable that especially blue colour terms such as *blo* (ON), *blew* (OF), *asure* (OF), *inde* (OF), *pers* (OF), *pale* (OF), and red colour terms such as *sanguin* (OF), *scarlet* (OF), *crimson* (OF), *vermilion* (OF), *vermlet* (OF) were adopted. In addition to them, in Modern English, the vocabulary of other colour terms greatly increased with the development of civilisation and gradually detailed colouring became possible.'[1] If Emily Brontë's colour words can be regarded as those of the author representative of the 19th century when historically, a system of present English had established, the world reflected by them seems monochrome based on tones of black and white rather than of garish colour.

When I arranged colour words of *Jane Eyre* in the same way as those of *Wuthering Heights* according to the frequency of use of 11 kinds of basic colour words such as 'white,' 'black,' 'red,' 'yellow,' 'green,' 'blue,' 'brown,' 'purple,' 'pink,' 'orange' and 'grey' which Mr Sukagawa lists, the result was 'black'(81 times), 'white' (69), 'blue'(30), 'green'(26), 'grey'(22), 'red'(20), 'brown'(19), 'purple' (16), 'red-room'(11), 'pink'(8), 'blackened'(5), 'yellow'(5), 'whitewashed'(3), 'blackness'(2), 'pearl-grey'(2), 'raven-black'(2), 'redness' (2), 'silver-white'(2), 'silver-white'(2), 'blackaviced,' 'blackberries,' 'blacker,' 'blacksmith,' 'blood-red,' 'bluebeard,' 'blue-eyed,' 'blue-piled,' 'bluer,' 'dark-blue,' 'death-white,' 'greener,' 'green-hollow,' 'greenness,' 'grey-headed,' 'moss-blackened,' 'red-haired,' 'sea-blue,' 'shoot-black,' 'silver-grey,' 'silver-grey,' 'sky-blue,' 'whiteness,' 'whiter.' I treated partially 'black' and 'white' descriptive of the main characters in this article and referred mainly to which character each colour was used for, what it modified and what it indicated.

To begin with, the examples of Jane Eyre are seen most frequently.

(1) I had brushed *my black* stuff travelling dress, prepared

my bonnet, gloves, and muff; (104)[2]

(2) However, when I had brushed my hair very smooth, and put on my *black* frock – (114)

(3) a *black* merino cloak, a *black* beaver bonnet; (131)

(4) however, I repaired to my room, and, with Mrs Fairfax's aid, replaced my *black* stuff dress by one of *black* silk; (136)

(5) With infinite difficulty, for he was stubborn as a stone, I persuaded him to make an exchange in favour of a sober *black* satin and pearl-grey silk. (301)

(6) ' ⋯ you may make a dressing-gown for yourself out of the pearl-grey silk, and an infinite series of waistcoats out of the *black* satin.' (301)

(7) It was enough that in yonder closet, opposite my dressing-table, garments said to be hers had already displaced my *black* stuff Lowood frock and straw bonnet: (308)

(8) eddying darkness seemed to swim round me, and reflection came in as *black* and confused a flow. (331)

(9) My *black* silk frock hung against the wall. (381)

(10) and the strange little figure there gazing at me, with a *white* face and arms specking the gloom, and glittering eyes of fear moving where all else was still, had the effect of a real spirit: (21)

(11) and adjusted my clean *white* tucker, I thought I should do respectably enough to appear before Mrs Fairfax; (114)

(12) How would a *white* or a pink cloud answer for a gown, do you think? (299)

(13) 'I will leave you by yourself, *white* dream,' I said. (308)

(14) a *white* December storm had whirled over June; (330)

(15) I see a *white* cheek and a faded eye, but no trace of tears. (336)

The above 'black' or 'white' describes (1) 'stuff travelling dress,' (2) 'frock,' (3) 'merino cloak,' 'beaver bonnet,' (4) 'stuff dress,' 'stuff dress of silk,' (5) 'satin dress,' (6) 'waistcoat out of the satin' (7) 'stuff Lowood frock,' (8) 'flow' and (9) 'silk frock,' (10) 'face,' (11) 'tucker,' (12) 'cloud,' (13) 'dream,' (14) 'December storm' and (15) 'cheek.'

The examples in (1)(2)(3)(4)(5)(6)(7)(9)(11)(12)(13) are descriptive of clothes, and the author directs her attention especially to describing Jane's clothes. Clothes in (1)(2)(3)(4)(5)(6)(7)(9) are divided, according to the material of Jane's clothes: one is 'stuff dress,' 'merino cloak, ' 'stuff frock' and 'beaver bonnet.' The OED defines 'stuff' as 'a textile fabric' and 'a woollen fabric,' and *Oxford Advanced Learner's Dictionary* defines 'merino' as 'the wool of the merino sheep or a fabric made from this wool, used for making clothes.' To borrow words from the dictionaries and to sum up, Jane usually liked to wear garments made of woollen fabric and a hat made of beaver's fur, or material resembling the fur of a beaver. The textures which contrast them are 'silk' and 'satin.' The scenes (4), (5), (6) and (9) where the 'silk' and 'satin' are used indicate the clothes which Jane put on for her wedding to Mr Rochester. They are the ones which Jane finally persuaded Rochester who tried to choose only brilliant and rich clothes, and decided reluctantly. Throughout the novel, Jane is described as a person who is quietly dressed and has no confidence in her appearance. We can often encounter scenes where Jane complains about her own ugliness. It is often said that Jane Eyre was the one who reflected the author Charlotte and 'Charlotte was worried about her own ugliness.'[3] It is considered that by using sober colours centred on 'black,' Charlotte tried to contrast a Jane Eyre or Charlotte with noblemen and noblewomen described by gorgeous and elegant clothes based on mainly 'white.'

The *OED* defines (11) 'tucker' as 'a piece of lace or the like, worn by women within or around the top of bodice in the 17-18th c.; a frill of lace worn round the neck,' and quotes 'some of the girls have two clean *tuckers* in the week; .. the rules limit them to one' from chapter vii as the fourth example of the above-mentioned meaning. In other words, (11) is descriptive of white clothes worn under 'black frock.'

(12) is a metaphor and indicates Jane Eyre's ideal gown which Mr Rochester was asking Adèle about. (13) is also a metaphor for Jane Eyre's wedding dress.

(10)(15) are of Jane's facial parts. (10) indicates an incident in the red-room; Jane's figure reflected in its mirror, and whiteness of cheek in (15) indicate Jane's pale or poor complexion after Jane found their marriage had broken down.

(8) indicates Jane after her marriage had ended. 'Reflecting on her marriage to Mr Rochester' is compared to 'a black and confused flow.'

(14) indicates a state of Jane's mind when Mr Rochester's and Jane's marriage was broken down by Mr Mason's appearance.

The examples with the second-highest frequency are of Edward Fairfax Rochester. 'Rochester is said to be modelled on Constantin Heger who was headmaster at the Maison d'Education pour les Jeunes Demoiselles in Brussels, Belgium where Charlotte went to qualify as a French teacher."[4]

(16) his square forehead, made squarer by the horizontal sweep of his *black* hair. (137)

(17) his *black* eyes darted sparks. (233)

(18) I took a soft *black* pencil, gave it a broad point, and worked away. (262)

(19) of course, some *black* whiskers were wanted, and some jetty hair, tufted on the temples, and waved above the forehead. (262)

(20) And now he unknit his *black* brows; (294)

(21) His eye, as I have often said, was a *black* eye: (325)

(22) 'Just to comb out this shaggy *black* mane. ···' (486)

Each 'black' modifies (16)'hair,' (17)'eyes,' (18)'pencil,' (19)'whiskers,' (20) 'brows,' (21) 'eye' and (22) 'mane.' (16)(17)(19)(20)(21)(22) are all related to Rochester's face. The earliest meaning of 'mane' is 'long hair on the back of the neck and the shoulders, characteristic of various animals, esp. the horse and lion' and then it was applied to the human and began to have the meaning of 'a person's long hair'(OED). The author devotes her attention to the description of his face, and it seems to put emphasis on his natural darkness.

In (18), 'black' is used to describe the pencil which Jane took to draw Mr Rochester's portrait.

Bertha Antoinetta Mason Rochester is Mr Rochester's mad wife.

(23) the long dishevelled hair, the swelled *black* face, the

exaggerated stature, were figments of imagination; (319)

(24) *black* clouds were casting up over it; (346)

(25) ' … When I think of the thing which flew at my throat this morning, hanging its *black* and scarlet visage over the nest of my dove, my blood curdles − ' (348)

(26) "… but without, I am perfectly aware, lies at my feet a rough tract to travel, and around me gather *black* tempests to encounter." (352)

(27) She was a big woman, and had long, *black* hair: (476)

(28) approaching one of the small, *black* doors, he put it in the lock; (235)

(29) the low, *black* door, opened by Mr Rochester's master key, admitted us to the tapestried room, with its great bed, and its pictorial cabinet. (327)

'Black' modifies (23) 'face,' (24) 'clouds,' (25) 'visage,' (26) 'tempests,' (27) 'hair' and (28)(29) 'door' respectively. The *OED* defines 'visage' as 'the face, the front part of the head, of a person (rarely of an animal),' and cites 'the maniac bellowed: she parted her shaggy locks from her *visage*' from chapter xxvi in *Jane Eyre* as the 17th example of the above-stated meaning. To sum up, Charlotte take an interest in Bertha's 'face' and 'hair.' 'Black' is characteristic of Bertha and she is also 'a Creole who was born and raised in the West Indies,'[5] and so it turns out from it that one of a Creole's apparent features is to have a dark skin.

(24) and (26) are metaphor to Bertha or her surroundings. 'Black clouds' in (24) seems to suggest a dark premonition of what will happen to Mr Rochester in the near future as well as a rain

79

cloud before a storm in the sea in the West Indies. 'Black tempests' in (26) compares Bertha to the tempest which brings down evil as well as 'black clouds' in (24). 'Charlotte is said to draw inspiration for Bertha from seeing the attic where a madwoman had been locked in the 18th century, when Charlotte was governess to the Sidgwick family and visited Norton Conyers near Ripon.'[6]

(28) and (29) indicate, respectively, the door leading the room of Bertha and the room in which Bertha stabbed Mason. 'Black' in (28) (29) produces a queer atmosphere rather than a mere decrepitness since they are used for the room where Bertha was locked.

Mother Bunches is a gypsy fortuneteller who visited Thornfield when a dinner party was held there.

(30) She had on a red cloak and a *black* bonnet: (221)
(31) she was bending over the fire, and seemed reading in a little *black* book, like a prayer-book, by the light of the blaze: (221)
(32) she then drew out a short *black* pipe, and lighting it, began to smoke. (222)
(33) She again put her short, *black* pipe to her lips and renewed her smoking with vigour. (222)
(34) elf-locks bristled out from beneath a *white* band which passed under her chin, and came half over her cheeks or rather jaws; (221)

'Black' or 'white' describes (30) 'bonnet,' (31) 'book,' (32)(33) 'pipe' and (34) 'band.' 'Black' is characteristic of Mother Bunches, and so only 'white' modifying (34) 'band' is striking.

St John Rivers is the minister of the parish at Morton.

(35) What business had I to approach the *white* door, or touch the glittering knocker? (367)

(36) She shook her head, she 'was sorry she could give me no information', and the *white* door closed, quite gently and civilly: (367)

(37) I could see a clock, a *white* deal table, some chairs. (372)

(38) As I looked at his lofty forehead, still and pale as a *white* stone – (438)

(39) a sort of raw curate, half strangled with his *white* neck-cloth, and stilted up on his thick-soled high-lows, eh? (490)

Each 'white' describes (35)(36) 'door,' (37) 'deal table,' (38) 'stone' and (39) 'neck-cloth.' (35)(36)(37) are of St John Rivers's house, and it is called Moor House. (38)(39) are of St John Rivers. 'White' contrastive to 'black' indicating Mr Rochester is used for St John.

Mr Brocklehurst is 'the minister of Brocklebridge Church and son of Naomi Brocklehurst, founder of Lowood School.'[7]

(40) a *black* pillar! (40)

(41) A long stride measured the schoolroom, and presently beside Miss Temple, who herself had risen, stood the same *black* column which had frowned on me so ominously from the hearth-rug of Gateshead. (73)

(42) 'My dear children,' pursued the *black* marble clergyman,

with pathos, 'this is a sad, a melancholy occasion; (78)

'Black' describes (40) 'pillar,' (41) 'column' and (42) 'marble clergyman' respectively. What is common to 'pillar,' 'column' and 'marble' are 'hardness' and 'coldness,' considering from them, the author seems to have implanted 'rigid' image in Mr Brocklehurst. 'He is thought to be modelled on Rev. William Carus Wilson, a founder of the Clergy Daughters' School at Cowan Bridge where Charlotte went with Emily. There seemed the fact that Mr Wilson walked the pupils including Charlotte on every Sunday to Mr Wilson's church at Tunstall about 10 kilo distant.[8] On the ground that Charlotte felt the event to be agony, it is natural that she tried to project Mr Wilson into Mr Brocklehurst.

Maria Temple is the superintendent and music teacher of Lowood; she conducts herself with such grace, self-confidence, and purity that she becomes Jane's idol.[9]

> (43) her dress, also in the mode of the day, was of purple cloth, relieved by a sort of Spanish trimming of *black* velvet; (57)
> (44) (where I was well contented to stand, for I derived a child's pleasure from the contemplation of her face, her dress, her one or two ornaments, her *white* forehead, her clustered and shining curls, and beaming dark eyes) (84)
> (45) Close by Miss Temple's bed, and half covered with its *white* curtains, there stood a little crib. (93)

The aforesaid 'black' or 'white' modifies (43) 'velvet,' (44) 'forehead' and (45) 'curtains.' The *OED* explains that 'velvet' is 'a textile fabric of silk having a short, dense, and smooth piled surface,' and quotes 'I had on my *black velvet* because it was mourning' from a letter by E. RUSKIN in 1851 as the first instance of 'a velvet dress.' Apart from the fact that Charlotte's instance is 4 years earlier but it is not adopted in the *OED*, 'a velvet dress' is thought to have become popular since this time.

Mrs Fairfax is 'the housekeeper at Thornfield; she is also a distant relative of Rochester by marriage.'[10]

(46) I saw her in a *black* gown and widow's cap; (103)

(47) an arm-chair high-backed and old-fashioned, wherein sat the neatest imaginable little elderly lady, in widow's cap, *black* silk gown and snowy muslin apron; (110)

(48) Mrs Fairfax assumed her best *black* satin gown, her gloves, and her gold watch; (188)

Each 'black' describes (46) 'gown,' (47) 'silk gown' and (48) 'satin gown.' The 'silk and satin gown' convey a high-class impression. She is actually described as 'a female who fills the role which the other employees are not entrusted as she maintains the house during its master Rochester's frequent absences. She is also described as a motherlike affectionate character different from the other high-class ladies who came to a house party at Thornfield Hall, such as Blanche Ingram.

Richard (Dick) Mason is a West Indies merchant and Bertha Mason's elder brother.

(49) An inaudible reply escaped Mason's *white* lips. (325)

(50) sister of this resolute personage, who is now, with his quivering limbs and *white* cheeks, showing you what a stout heart men may bear. (326)

(51) I had, again and again, held the water to Mason's *white* lips; (238)

'White' modifies (49) 'lips,' (50) 'cheeks' and (51) 'lips' each. Whiteness of his lips and cheeks indicate his facial appearance after Mr Mason was stabbed by Bertha.

Bessie is the servant at Gateshead Hall and the only person who treated small Jane tenderly at Gateshead Hall.

(52) I remember her as a slim young woman, with *black* hair, dark eyes, very nice features, and good, clear complexion; (38)

(53) very good looking, with *black* hair and eyes, and lively complexion. (104)

Each 'black' modifies (52) 'hair' and (53) 'hair and eyes.'

Miss Scatcherd is 'the sharp-tongued, mean teacher of history and grammar at Lowood, and repeatedly punishes and humiliates Helen Burns.'[11] Miss Scatcherd is also modelled on a real person at Clergy Daughters' School at Cowan Bridge.[12]

(54) the little one with *black* hair is Miss Scatcherd; (61)

(55) Do you like the little *black* one, and the Madame – ? (61)

'Black' modifies (54) 'hair' and (55) 'one(=teacher)' respectively.

Grace Poole is the employee who feeds and cares for Bertha

Antoinetta Mason Rochester.

> (56) There she sat, staid and taciturn-looking, as usual, in her brown stuff gown, her check apron, *white* handkerchief, and cap. (175)
>
> (57) This was when I chanced to see the third story staircase door (which of late had always been kept locked) open slowly, and give passage to the form of Grace Poole, in prim cap, *white* apron, and handkerchief; (187)

Each 'white' modifies (56) 'handkerchief' and (57) 'apron.' They are what Grace Poole wore, and 'white' is used for her but by contrast, 'black' is used for Bertha. Jane was informed that it was an employee Grace Poole who let out strange laughter. But what Jane saw was aspect quite different from Grace Poole's one. Charlotte seems to make a weird impression on readers by using the contrasting colours.

To conclude, it is judged from this research that Charlotte intends to distinguish favourite persons from hateful ones because she wrote this work, conscious of her readership, and such preference is also reflected by use of colours. It is also a distinctive feature that more 'black' tend to be connected with definite characters than 'white.'

Notes

1 Seizo Sukagawa, 1999. *A Historical Study of English Color Terms — Meaning, Metaphor and Symbolism —*. Tokyo: Seibido. pp.12-15.

2　Charlotte Brontë, 1996. *Jane Eyre*. London: Penguin Books Ltd. All the quotations are from this edition.
3　Seiko Aoyama, 1984. *Charlotte Brontë's Journey*. Tokyo: Kenkyusha. p.123.
4　Yoshitsugu Uchida, 1998. *The Brontës*. Tokyo: Kenkyusha. p.10, 135.
5　Hiroshi Nakaoka, Yoshitsugu Uchida, 1997. *Brontë Shimai no Jiku*. Tokyo: Hokuseido. p.41.
6　Yoshitsugu Uchida *op. cit.*, p.7.
7　Mary Ellen Snodgrass, 1999. *Cliffs Notes on Brontë's Jane Eyre*. Lincoln: Cliffs Notes, Inc. p.11.
8　Phyllis Bentley, 1969. *The Brontës*. London: Thames and Hudson Ltd. p.26.
9　Mary Ellen Snodgrass, *op. cit.*, p.11.
10 Mary Ellen Snodgrass, *op. cit.*, p.11.
11 Mary Ellen Snodgrass, *op. cit.*, p.15.
12 Phyllis Bentley, *op. cit.*, p.26.

"Kinde" and Related Terms in John Gower's *Confessio Amantis*

Masahiko Kanno

The common phrase *be weie of kinde* (34 exx. in all),[1] of which Gower makes frequent employments, may serve seemingly as a mere line-filler or rhyme-tag, but the most complex words *kinde* (OE. *-cund* 'of the nature of') and *nature* (L.*natura* < *nasci* 'to be born,' from which derive *nation, native, innate*, etc.), the respective derivatives of which play an important role in the *Confessio Amantis*.[2] The study of these words will be sure to reveal part of Gower's world-view or *Weltanschauung*. Genius, the priest of Venus, depends his ethical and moral standard of judgment or decision mostly on whether man's love or murder in the stories is "kinde" or "unkinde." As a general rule, various crimes against nature which man is liable to commit will be dealt with as some main themes in the *Confessio*. Accordingly, it was pertinent for Gower to have chosen Genius as a confessor, because Amans is so confused that he does not realize what he is. He has lost, in a literal sense, "genius," which means creativity and procreativity. Thus Amans strives to restore his true identity through making the confession to Genius.[3] "Kindeschipe" (2 exx.), "kinde, kynde" (224 exx.), and "kindely, kindly" (5 exx.) are words exploited frequently throughout the entire *Confessio*.

I repeat, ME. *kinde* plays a significant role in Gower's stories, specifically in those of love and murder. On the other hand, Gower uses some negative words, such as "unkinde, unkynde" (29 exx.), "unkendenesse" (3 exx.), "unkindeschipe" (10 exx.), "unkindeliche, unkindely" (6 exx.), and "unkendeli" (1 ex.) to judge an unreasonable, brutal or immoral conduct or behaviour in terms of the ethical or moral point of view. God gave beasts "kinde," suggesting the natural instincts, desires, or feelings within animal, while God gave man "reson," suggesting the intellectual power or faculty, by which he should control "kinde." The ordered Christian universe is a world governed and controlled by reason. G.R. Coffman remarks that "The rule of reason is the basic element in his conception of an ordered universe. The use of this God-given intellectual power will, he is convinced, result in a world of peace and harmony, in proper human relations, in worthy rulers, and in prosperous England."[4]

It is reason that forbids man to act by impulse, or to slay or treat prisoners cruelly like beasts even in war. Lovers have to restrain their blind passion by good reason, avoid committing crimes, and aim at their marriage as a goal of love. Gower wished marriage to be one of the solutions of the dilemma between amorous passion and reason.

"Nature," adopted from L. *natura*, is a synonym for Gk. *physis*. G.D. Economou declares that "Natura, therefore, involves the history of ideas and literary forms or, to put it more accurately, the history of the mutations of certain ideas and forms as they were appropriated and used by thinkers and writers of successive generations and periods."[5]

In fact, "kinde" and nature, which are full of shades of multiple meaning, are a great problem worthy of writing a book, but I shall give the outlines of the pregnant word *kinde* and its kindred terms roughly, not systematically, and then examine their meanings in the context of the stories proper concretely.

1. God is called "the hihe makere of nature" (2.916), and sometimes "The hihe makere of natures" (7.1508) in the plural, which may be due to the requirement of the rhyme. "Makere" means, of course, the Creator of the universe. God is also called "The creatour of alle kinde" (7.994) or "the hihe creatour of thinges" (6.1789) in the plural.

Pan (cf. "panic") is "the god of kinde" (8.2239), which is the Greek god of shepherds and of nature. "In later times from association of his name with τὸ πᾶν the all, everything, the universe," explains the *OED*, "he was considered as an impersonation of Nature, of which his attributes were taken as mysterious symbols." Chaucer identifies Pan with "god of kynde" (*BD*. 511), first cited in the *OED*. Bacchus is called "god of nature" (5.1041), who is the god of wine, glossed as "Bachus deus vini" in the *marginalia*.

Like Chaucer's depiction of nature in the *Parlement of Foules*, Gower inroduces the goddess of nature into the *Confessio* to announce the advent of spring. Nature appears as a personified figure. In spring, she adorns field and meadow sumptuously with all sorts of pretty flowers, and covers wood and forest with green leaves, so that the birds may hide themselves amid them:

>Bot whan the wynter goth away,
>And that *Nature the goddesse*
>Wole of hir oughne fre largesse
>With herbes and with floures bothe
>The feldes and the medwes clothe,
>And ek the wodes and the greves
>Ben heled al with grene leves,
>So that a brid hire hyde mai,
>Betwen Averil and March and Maii. (5.5960-68)

In the *Mirour de l'Omme*, Nature is personified as "la deesce Nature":

>Et c'estoit en le temps joly
>Du Maii, quant *la deesce Nature*
>Bois, champs et prées de sa verdure
>Reveste, et l'oisel front leur cry,
>Chantant deinz ce buisson flori. (939-43)
>
>(And it was in the pretty time of May, when the goddess Nature reclothes wood, field, and meadow with her verdure, and the birds make their songs, singing in the flowering bush.)[6]

Gower sketches roughly the Goddess Nature as "Maistress In kinde," who teaches all living beings on earth without "lawe positif" — for which she takes no "charge" or responsibility — and exercises her laws without restraints. For example, Canace and Macharius, bound by a spell, were suddenly overwhelmed with desires and then committed the horrible sin of incest. Gower makes an exploit of the clever means of settling a trouble, such as enchantment or a kind of magic, in order to avert the shocking occurrence of incest between a brother and a sister, towards whom Gower is amazingly sympathetic":

> And after *sche which is Maistresse*
> *In kinde* and techeth every lif
> Withoute lawe positif,
> Of which sche takth nomaner charge,
> Bot kepth hire lawes al at large,
> *Nature*, tok hem into lore
> And tawht hem so, that overmore
> Sche hath hem in such wise daunted,
> That thei were, as who seith, enchaunted. (3.170-78)

"Maistresse" is used allegorically to refer to "a sovereign lady, ruler, or queen." She is her own arbiter.

Natural law was first exemplified by the universal sexual instinct. God's injunction was "Be fruitful and increase," as recorded in Genesis, 1.28:

> And in the *lawe* a man mai finde,
> Hou god to man *be weie of kinde*
> Hath set the world to *multeplie*;
> And who that wol him justfie,
> It is ynouh to do the lawe. (5.6421-25)

Kurt Olsson notes that "Amans seems to take a firm 'theological' stand, introducing a Biblical text [i.e. the lawe (5.6421)] to challenge the priest's defense of virginity."[7] It is familiar that Chaucer has The Wife of Bath protest against the priority of virginity to marriage: "God bad us for to wexe and multiplye" (*WBP*, 28).

The goddess Nature rules all living beings under the moon. The force or "kindly lust," which brings into existence everything in the universe, is apotheosized as a goddess. "In one important particular," G.G. Fox asserts, "Gower's view of nature closely resembles that of Alanus de Insulis — his intimate connection of nature with sex and procreation".[8]

> For *Nature* is under the Mone
> Maistresse of every lives kinde,
> Bot if so be that sche mai finde
> Som holy man that wol withdrawe
> His *kindly lust* ayein hir lawe;
> Bot sielde whanne it falleth so,
> For fewe men ther ben of tho,
> Bot of these othre ynowe be,
> Whiche of here oghne nycete
> Ayein *Nature* and hire office
> Deliten hem in sondri vice,
> Wherof that sche fulofte hath pleigned,
> And ek my Court it hath desdeigned
> And evere schal. (8.2330-43)

The traditional theme of the complaint of Nature is apparent in the phrase "sche fulofte hath pleigned" of "sondri vice."[9] Nature always complains of particularly homo-sexuality. It is remarkable that sexual abstinence even in the case of holy man is against the law of nature.

Gower's obvious concern was with the union of male and female, sexual desire, and marriage:

> The Madle is mad for the femele,
> Bot where as on desireth fele,
> That nedeth noght *be weie of kinde*. (7.4215-17)

It is not "be weie of kinde" that a man desires many women.

The rape of Lucrece is concerned literally with rape. Arrons, a tyrannical knight, made advances to Lucrece, the wife of Collatin. He would call to mind amorously her graceful face and figure moulded by Nature. Suddenly she was sexually assaulted:

> The softe pas and forth he ferde
> Unto the bed wher that sche slepte,
> Al sodeinliche and in he crepte,
> And hire in bothe his Armes tok. (7.4970-73)

The feminine features are formed by Nature, which is also personified as the goddess Nature:

> Ferst the fetures of hir face,
> In which *nature* hadde alle grace
> Of wommanly beaute beset,
> So that it myhte noght be bet. (7.4877-80)

Chaucer presents the goddess Nature as the creator of beautiful women, which goes back to antiquity. The most familiar description is found in Chaucer's *The Physician's Tale*:[10]

> For *Nature* hath with sovereyn diligence
> Yformed hire in so greet excellence,
> As though she wolde seyn, "Lo! I, *Nature*,
> Thus kan I forme and peynte a creature,
> Whan that me list; who kan me countrefete?" (9-13)

"Kinde" means "birth":

> So wot I nothing *after kinde*
> Where I mai gentilesse finde. (4.2255-56)

Genius declares definitely that "gentilesse" has nothing to do with "kinde" in the sense of birth. The phrase *after kinde* implies "in keeping with birth."

"Nature" means "gifts of nature" (a heredity, birth, hereditary circumstance; kinship by blood), as contrasted to the gifts of grace (fortune, and education; inherited inclination, instinct):

> And thus *nature* his pourveance
> Hath mad for man to liven hiere;
> Bot god, which hath the Soule diere,
> Hath formed it in other wise. (7.490-93)

Both "nature" and "kynde" below mean "essential character,

an inherent quality," as in "Morpheus, the whos *nature/* Is forto take the figure/ Of what persone that him liketh" (4.3039). "Morpheus" [Gr. μορφή 'form'] is the god of dreams, which is Ovid's name, popularly often taken as the god of sleep. "The world as *of his propre kynde/* Was evere untrewe" (Prol.534). The *OED* takes "nature" to mean "the essential qualities," as in "Upon the *nature* of the vice" (6.531) and "Scorpio..Which *of his kinde* is moiste and cold" (7.1133). The *MED* takes "nature(s" to mean "an inherent quality, attribute(s, as in "He clepeth god the ferste cause.. Of which that every creature/ Hath his beinge and his *nature*" (7.90), "Of everychon/ That ben of bodely substance,/ The *nature* and the circumstance/ Thurgh this science it is ful soght" (7.142), and "Bot yit the lawe original,/ Which he hath set in the *natures* [of the planets],/ Mot worchen in the creatures..Bot if it stonde upon miracle" (7.659). "Nature" means "a field of learning," as in "The *nature* of Philosophie (7.24-25) and "These thre sciences hath divided/ And the *nature* also decided" (7.50-52). "Natures" means "family, race." The *OED* takes "natures" to mean "a thing or person of a particular quality or character:

> The god commandeth the *natures*
> That thei to him obeien alle. (7.108-9)

"Kinde" is used in proverb, meaning "nature":

> For in Phisique this I finde,
> Usage is the *seconde kinde*. (6.663-64)

95

"Kinde" means "mankind," as in "I thenke ..speke of thing../ Which every *kinde* hath upon honde" (1.11). Kurt Olsson emphasizes that "His (Gower's) first concern, however, is with sexual desire or the love that 'every *kinde* hath upon honde'."[11] "Kinde" means "a class of creatures," as in "The *kinde* of alle brides../ And ../The *kinde* of alle bestes" (1.2826, 282) and "the *kinde* of man" (5.2). "Kinde of man" means "the human race, mankind." "Kinde" means "sex," as in "of alle *kinde*/ Of women is thunsemlieste" (1.1624).

"Kinde" means "action habitual to a person, animal, etc., way." It is "kinde" or habit for the dog to bark at man behind:

> For as it is an houndes *kinde*
> To berke upon a man behinde,
> Riht so behinde his brother bak
> With false wordes whiche he spak
> He hath do slain, and that is rowthe. (2.1795-99)

Also it is not a habit for the dog to eat chaff:

> Thogh it be noght the houndes *kinde*
> To ete chaf, yit wol he werne
> An Oxe which comth to the berne,
> Therof to take eny fode. (2.84-87)

Similarly it is a habit for the dung-beetle to feast on filth (2.413), for all animals, including man, to have sex (4.1299-1301), and for the nightingale to "slepen al the nyght with open ye" (10), as described in the Prologue to the *Canterbury Tales*:

> I thenke upon the nyhtingale,
> Which slepeth noght *be weie of kinde*
> For love, in bokes as I finde. (4.2872-74)

"Kinde" means "sexual organs, testicles":

> For thus the wise clerkes telle,
> That no spirit bot of malice
> *Be weie of kinde* upon a vice
> Is tempted, and be such a weie
> Envie hath *kinde* put aweie
> And of malice hath his steringe. (2.3136-41)

According to Echard and Fanger, "Envy, of course, is destructive of desire. But Envy is also a sin against Nature and a sin with no natural cause; "Envie hath kinde put aweie"; so Nature's parts naturally, if unkindiy, fail the man consumed by envy."[12]

"Kinde" below may also apply to the sexual organ of penis:

> And ek he brenneth so withinne,
> That *kinde* mai no profit winne,
> Wherof he scholde his love plese. (2.3119-21)

"Nature, " governed by law, is used as a quasi-personified creator to whom man is indebted. Even when man has to obey nature, he should abstain from doing cruel act. "Nature" here means "instinct, sexual passion, or desire":

> The reddour oghte be restreigned
> To him that mai no bet aweie,
> Whan he mot to *nature* obeie.
> For it is seid thus overal,
> That nedes mot that nede schal
> Of that a lif doth *after kinde*,
> Wherof he mai no bote finde. (3.348-54)

No man can escape the impulse of love in nature:

> Whanne every brid upon his lay
> Among the griene leves singeth,
> And love of his pointure stingeth
> *After the lawes of nature*
> The youthe of every creature. (7.1046-50)

Fox suggests that "Gower regards homo-sexuality with abhorrence, not because it is against the *lex positiva*, but because it is against the law of nature."[13]

> For love hateth nothing more
> Than thing which stant ayein the lore
> Of that *nature* in *kinde* hath sett. (4.493-95)

"'Lex positiva' is opposed to 'lex Dei' and 'lex naturalis.' In the days of Gower," remarks E.W. Stockton, "the churches abused their religious authority too much 'ad eorum lucrum,' so that 'lex positiva' was censured as the evil law. In *Vox Clamantis* Gower criticizes bitterly the clergy who force severe 'lex positiva' on persons: Lex etenim Cristi fuit hec quam gracia mulcet,/ Nostra set ex penis lex positiua riget (*VC*, 3.255-56)."[14]

"Al erthli thing" was created in order to serve man, while God created the Soul for the purpose of serving and pleasing Him. All the beasts on earth serve "her oghne kinde," while the Soul ministers to "reson":

> Al erthli thing which god began
> Was only mad to serve man;
> Bot he the Soule al only made
> Himselven forto serve and glade.
> Alle othre bestes that men finde
> Thei serve unto here oghne *kinde*,
> Bot to *reson* the Soule serveth;
> Wherof the man his thonk deserveth
> And get him with hise werkes goode
> The perdurable lyves foode. (7.511-20)

"Kinde" means "instinct or desire." Genius lays stress on a sharp distinction between man and the beasts with which he shares the "lawe of kinde."

Gower employs the phrase *after the lawe of kinde* strictly in such a scientific and technical term as "according to the laws or principles governing the natural world":

> For as the point in a compas
> Stant evene amiddes, riht so was

> This erthe set and schal abyde,
> That it may swerve to no side,
> And hath his centre *after the lawe*
> *Of kinde*, and to that centre drawe
> Desireth every worldes thing,
> If ther ne were no lettyng. (7.229-36)

"Kindly" means "concordant with the laws or processes of nature, produced by nature, natural," as in "Virgo the nexte/ Of Signes cleped is..Be *kindly* disposicion/ Of dreie and cold this Maiden is" (7.1094).

"Unkindeli" implies "unhealthy, unwholesome, corrupt," which is used chiefly in a medical and physiological sense:

> For thilke blod which scholde have ese
> To regne among the moiste veines,
> Is drye of thilke *unkendeli* peines
> Thurgh whiche Envie is fyred ay. (2.3122-25)

"Be weie of kinde" implies "in the natural order or way of things":

> Bot nou the laste sterre of alle
> The tail of Scorpio men calle,
> Which to Mercurie and to Satorne
> *Be weie of kinde* mot retorne
> After the preparacion
> Of due constellacion. (7.1425-30)

Thus the elements and the planets are subject to "kinde."

"Kinde" means "the natural disposition or temperament of a person":

> He schal desire joie and merthe,
> Gentil, courteis and debonaire,
> To speke his wordes softe and faire,
> Such schal he *be weie of kinde*. (7.784-87)

The *MED* takes "be weie of kinde" to imply "naturally, by innate disposition." Thus human disposition like "gentil, courteis, debonaire," and so forth, is determined by nature, against the old adage: Gentle is that gentle does.

"Naturel" means "intrinsic, inherent":

> After the disposicioun
> Of *naturel* complexioun
> To sum womman it is plesance,
> That to an other is grevance. (1.1497-1500)

J.A.W. Bennett notes lines above 1497-8 as "according as Nature has arranged the blend of humours that produces one's temperament."[15]

2. The story of Midas (5.141-362) is intended to point a moral, which is an *exemplum* against the vice of Avarice. Midas "excedeth Mesure more than him nedeth" (5.247-48). Gower's view of moderation is emphasized here. Genius warns that a slave to gold is

against nature:

> It is to *kinde* no plesance
> That man above his sustienance
> Unto the gold schal serve and bowe,
> For that mai no *reson* avowe. (5.121-24)

"Reason [is] his other touchstone," as J.A.W. Bennett puts it.[16] "Sustienance" and "reson" are words which play a significant part in unfolding the story proper. All thing Midas touched turned to gold. When he would eat and drink by his physical nature, "His disch, his coppe, his drinke, and his mete" (5.285) to which he put his hand, turned to gold at once. No matter how hungry and thirsty he felt, he was unable to satisfy his hunger and quench his thirst:

> bot hunger ate laste
> Him tok, so that he moste nede
> *Be weie of kinde* his hunger fede. (5.280-82)

The sense of hunger or thirst is caused by a physical natural desire, which man cannot suppress by force of reason. Hunger has no law, as the proverb runs. The *MED* takes "be weie of kinde" to mean "in accordance with the natural process."

Midas learns a lesson: "gold..of his oghne kinde/ Is lasse worth than is the rinde/ To sustience of mannes fode" (5.323-25). "Rinde" means figuratively "the bark of a tree." Finally Genius urges the audience to "seche non encress/ Of gold, which is the breche of pes" (5.331-32).

3. In the familiar story of Ceix and Alceone (4.2927-3123), one of Gower's best-told stories, Dedalion, brother of Ceix, "the king of Trocinie" (4.2928), was transformed into a goshawk "per cas":

> Dedalion, and he per cas
> *Fro kinde* of man forschape was
> Into a Goshauk of liknesse. (4.2933-35)

"Kinde of man" or a human natural form is changed suddenly into an avian shape. Ceix and Alceone, changed into birds, "bringen forth of brides *kinde*" (4.3119).

4. Genius develops "unkindeschipe," an act ungrateful towards the parents. "Unkindeshipe" here means "an unfilial act." According to Gower, a man who will not know a good act is "unkinde." A man takes all that is given, and yet repays nothing, even if only one day is left until he dies. A man, who filled his barn with corn, is greedy to gain corn, and yet he is unwilling to give a single grain when he comes to:

> He takth what eny man wol yive,
> Bot whil he hath o day to live,
> He wol nothing rewarde ayein;
> He gruccheth forto yive o grein,
> Wher he hath take a berne full.
> That makth a *kinde* herte dull,

> To sette his trust in such *frendschipe*,
> Ther as he fint no *kindeschipe*; (5.4903-10)

It makes "a kinde herte" dull to believe in friendship without natural gratitude. Gower probably coined "kindeschipe" for the requirement of rhyme with "frendschipe."

"Kinde" means "generous, gracious, noble," which comes near to a modern sense of "kind":

> Thus hiere I many a man compleigne,
> That nou on daies thou schalt finde
> At nede fewe frendes *kinde*;
> What thou hast don for hem tofore,
> It is foryete, as it were lore. (5.4912-16)

The phrase *at nede...frendes* kinde implies "generous friends in time of need," which is equivalent to the proverb": A friend in need is a friend indeed."

The *MED* takes "nature" to refer to "Nature as an embodiment of moral and political principles." Nature condemns the vice of ingratitude, because "unkinde," often used as a basis for moral judgment, means an act done "ayein kinde":

> The bokes speken of this vice,
> And telle hou god of his justice,
> *Be weie of kinde* and ek *nature*
> And every lifissh creature,
> The lawe also, who that it kan,

Thei dampnen an *unkinde* man. (5.4917-22)

Both "kinde" and "nature" also mean "natural affection, parental or filial love." "Unkinde" means "ungrateful, unappreciative."

Genius explicitly defines the word *unkinde* as the act of "returning evil for good," which is by no means in keeping with "kinde":

> It is al on to seie *unkinde*
> As thing which don is *ayein kinde*,
> For it with *kinde* nevere stod
> A man to yelden evel for good.
> For who that wolde taken hede,
> A beste is glad of a good dede,
> And loveth thilke creature
> *After the lawe of his nature*
> Which doth him ese. (5.4923-31)

Even animals will be pleased with gentle treatment and feel deep affection to persons who give consolation to them "after the lawe of his nature." "The unnaturalness of ingratitude is evidenced by the behavior of the animals," as H. White points out.[17]

5. Genius tells the story of Adrian, a rich Roman lord, and Bardus, a poor ignorant peasant, as an *exemplum* against the sin of ingratitude. Both an ape and a serpent which Bardus escued from a deep pit did him a favor, but Adrian was ungrateful to Bardus, because Adrian broke his promise to give half his worldly goods in return for rescue. Humorously enough, the serpent bowed Bardus "in a serpent way":

> he sih beside
> The grete gastli Serpent glyde,
> Til that sche cam in his presence,
> And in hir *kinde* a reverence
> Sche hath him do. (5.5061-65)

"Kinde" means "a way, fashion." Gower brings out the instructive contrast between Adrian's threatening and unnatural way without saying "grant merci" (6.5028) and their kind and human way of greeting.

6. Another familiar interesting story of Theseus and Ariadne (5.5231-5495) is concerned with the *exemplum* against the vice of ingratitude. Theseus, son of Athene, fell in love with Ariadne, daughter of Minos. He is branded as "more than the beste unkinde" (5.5424) and "Fulfild of his unkindeschipe" (5.5427). She saved him from the danger of Minotaur, all of which he completely forgot. It was "a gret unkinde dede" (5.5479). What is worse, Theseus deserted Ariadne and then married her sister Fedra. This is a vice of "Unkindeschipe" (5.5485).

7. According to the *MED*, "kinde" means "having normal affections or disposition, well-disposed towards one's kin; also, dutiful, obedient":

> As sche that was gentil and *kinde*,
> In worschipe of hir Sostres mynde
> Sche made a riche enterement,
> For sche fond non amendement
> To syghen or to sobbe more. (5.5725-29)

"Kinde" are etymologically cognate with "gentil":

8. The unwritten law implanted in man's mind and heart, i. e. "the lawe which is naturel" (3.2581) is called "natural law," opposed to positive law. As provided by the natural law, no homicide shall exist in human society. Beasts do not devour the meat of their fellows. Even beasts have their own law to obey. It is a pity, indeed, that man who possesses instincts and, at the same time, is endowed with intellectual power, should kill his fellows. Even in time of war man is strictly forbidden to slaughter others:

> And sithen *kinde* hath such a weie,
> Thanne is it wonder of a man,
> Which *kynde* hath and *resoun* can,
> That he wol owther more or lasse
> His *kinde* and *resoun* overpasse,
> And sle that is to him semblable.
> So is the man noght *resonable*
> Ne *kinde*, and that is noght *honeste*,
> Whan he is worse than a beste. (3.2590-98)

"Man is, " writes H. White, "guided towards right moral action not only by a *kinde* external to him, but also by an internal *kinde* which is explicitly distinguished from human reason."[18] The adjective *kinde* implies "concordant with the natural moral law, lawful, moral," as in "the *kinde* love" (4.502).

In some cases, it is hard to make a rigid distinction between "kinde" and "resoun." The former comes near to the latter in the sense of "natural moral law." It is noteworthy that the adjective *kinde* (3.2597), listed as the first recorded example in the *MED*, means "concordant with the natural moral law, lawful, moral." Man is endowed with "kinde" and "resoun," but he deviates from it and kills his fellows. He is not reasonable, nor kind, nor honest. H.A. Klauser asserts that "Of one thing we can be certain: Gower does not think of reason and natural law as integrated because he speaks of them as two separate entities. Homicide, for example, is decried as an incredible violation of both man's *reson* and his *kinde*."[19]

9. The story of Iphis (4.451-529) is concerned with the mutation of a female into a male. From the start, Ligdus, Iphis' father, warned his wife that if she should bear a daughter, the baby would be deserted. In reality, she bore a daughter. Under such a harsh circumstance, his baby, in disguise of a son, had to survive:

> Forthi Cupide hath so besett
> His grace upon this aventure,
> That he *accordant to nature*,
> Whan that he syh the time best,
> That ech of hem hath other kest,

> Transformeth Iphne into a man,
> Wherof the *kinde* love he wan
> Of lusti yonge Iante his wif. (4.496–503)

The *MED* takes "love of kinde" to mean "fleshly love (as opposed to spiritual), "as in "love of kinde" (*TC*, 1.979). A remarkable thing is that the adjective *kinde*, as in "kinde love," means "concordant with the natural moral law, lawful moral," listed as the first recorded example in the *MED*. However, it bears a carnal connotation of "fleshly," since Iphne is changed into a man to have intercourse with his "lusti" young wife Iante.

10. Gower refers to the mysterious influence of kinship. As "nature" works the hereditary wonders that a child closely resembles a mother in face, the king Allee perceived in Moris the faint image of his wife Constance, though he had never recognized as his son. But the king did not know why he loved him on the spot instinctively, and he felt an affection or love, based on connection by blood. Such sympathy or compassion may be equal in meaning to "tacit understanding or telepathy":

> For *nature* as in resemblance
> Of face hem liketh so to clothe,
> That thei were of a suite bothe.
> The king was moeved in his thoght
> Of that he seth, and knoweth it noght;
> This child he *loveth kindely*,
> And yit he wot no cause why. (2.1376–82)

This is one of the three typical happenings in the story of Constance, where the word *kinde* occurs in the king Allee's recognition of his son. "Nature" means "the goddess Nature," who forms beautiful human face and figure, as mentioned above. "Kindely" means "owing to blood relationship."

The same idea is found in the story of Appollonius of Tyre (8.271-2008). King Appollonius sat quiet in the dark place. Then the harper named Thaise came to console and entertain him by singing to the harp. Though it was the first encounter between the father and his daughter Athenagoras, he loved her by instinct, since they were related by blood ("sibb of blood"):

> Bot of hem tuo a man mai liere
> What is to be so sibb of blod:
> Non wiste of other hou it stod,
> And yit the fader ate laste
> His herte upon this maide caste,
> That he hire *loveth kindely*,
> And yit he wiste nevere why. (8.1702-8)

Thus kinship mysteriously influences human beings. "Kindely" implies "owing to blood relationship."

11. The story of Calistona (5.6225-6358) is concerned with rape, which is told under the heading of "Robbery," because Jupiter robbed Calistona, king Lichaon's daughter, of her maidenhead. "Hire wombe aros and sche toswal" (5.6252). Diana noticed in bathing naked that Calistona became pregnant. Eventually she

bore a son named Archas. Then a jealous Juno was so angry that she transformed Calistona into a bear. Calistona saw her own son with a bow coming to hunt. She, who was transformed into a bear, approached him, since she herself was able to recognize him:

> For thogh sche hadde hire forme lore,
> The *love* was noght lost therfore
> Which *kinde* hath set under his *lawe*. (5.6321-23)

"Kinde" means "an affection or love owing to their blood relationship."

12. On a high mountain Tiresias (3.361-380) saw two serpents mating just as "nature hem tawhte." Then he stroke them with a staff. His act of striking was "unkinde" to nature. God was so angry that He transformed "unkindeliche" Tiresias, who once was a man, into a female figure, since he threw the normal order of nature into confusion. He did a harsh act to Nature:

> Upon an hih Montaine he [Tiresias] sih
> Tuo Serpentz in his weie nyh,
> And thei, so as *nature* hem tawhte,
> Assembled were, and he tho cawhte
> A yerde which he bar on honde,
> And thoghte that he wolde fonde
> To letten hem, and smot hem bothe:
> Wherof the goddes weren wrothe;

111

> And for he hath destourbed *kinde*
> And was so to *nature unkinde*,
> *Unkindeliche* he was transformed,
> That he which erst a man was formed
> Into a womman was forschape. (3.365-77)

"Nature" refers to the goddes Nature. As described earlier, she is "Maistresse/ In kinde and techeth every lif/ Withoute lawe positif,/ Of which sche takth nomaner charge" (3.170-73). As mentioned elsewhere, it is Nature itself that induced Canace and Mechaire to commit a sibling incest, because "What *nature* hath set in hir lawe/ Ther mai no mannes miht withdrawe" (3.355-56).

"Kinde" means "natural order of things" and "unkinde" (374) means "harsh, cruel, unkind." The last word *unkindeliche* means "in a manner contrary to the regular course of nature." Worthy of special mention is that "A more learned form of repetition, *traductio*, rings the changes on a root word," as John Burrow observed.[20]

Tiresias was punished for being harsh to nature. Accordingly, he was changed into a woman, because he did an act contrary to the regular course of nature. "Assembled," meaning "copulate, mate," is used euphemistically. It is unnatural for him to separate copulating snakes, since "he hath destourbed kinde/ And was so to nature unkinde" (3.373-74).

Man is superior to a beast. It might never been appropriate for a man to be angry at the two serpents mating according to "the teaching of nature, or instinct":

> More is a man than such a beste:

> So mihte it nevere ben honeste
> A man to wraththen him to sore
> Of that an other doth *the lore*
> *Of kinde*, in which is no malice,
> Bot only that it is a vice:
> And thogh a man be resonable,
> Yit *after kinde* he is menable
> To love, wher he wole or non. (3.383-91)

Gower makes Genius remark additionally that there is no malice nor ill-will in "kinde" itself, except that it is merely a vice or evil. Despite his will or intention, man has a natural propensity to fall in love. Even if he strives to be reasonable, he is inclined to be tempted naturally into love. "After kinde" means "by nature, naturally."

13. The story of Achilles and Deidamia (5.2961-3201) is told to point a moral against the vice of false witness and perjury. In fact, Achilles was not willing to disguise himself as a woman, but was forced to by his mother Thetis for the sake of saving his life. Achilles in disguise had Deidamia to his bed-fellow at night:

> Wher *kinde* wole himselve rihte,
> After the Philosophres sein,
> Ther mai no wiht be therayein:
> And that was thilke time seene.
> The longe nyhtes hem betuene
> *Nature*, which mai noght forbere,

> Hath mad hem bothe forto stere:
> Thei kessen ferst, and overmore
> The hihe weie of loves lore
> Thei gon, and al was don in dede,
> Wherof lost is the maydenhede. (5.3058-68)

J.A.W. Bennett declares that "an awareness of these forces [i.e. natural impulses] pervades every love-tale that Gower tells, and even determines his choice of such an *exemplum* as the story of Achilles and Deidamia."[21]

"Kinde" means "the natural instincts, desires." "Nature" (3063) also implies passion which no man can withstand. "Kinde" and "nature" are synonymously employed. The *OED* takes "rihte" to mean "to vindicate, set right, justify," while the *MED* takes it to mean "to govern, rule".

14. The Confessor urges a king to restrain "The fleisschly lustes of nature." "Kinde" should be served and at the same time "the lawe of god" observed, as referred to again in the story of Thobias and Sara. The importance of the virtue of "mesure" is frequently repeated throughout the work:

> Wherof a king schal modefie
> The fleisschly lustes of *nature*,
> Nou thenk I telle of such mesure,
> That bothe *kinde* schal be served
> And ek *the lawe of god* observed. (7.4210-14)

"Nature" means "sexual urge." It is hard to satisfy "kinde" and simultaneously make it accordant to reason, but Gower does not refer to specifically the manner how a king should behave himself.

A similar idea is repeated in Aristotle's letter to Alexander, in which the former advises the latter to observe moderation in lust, to satisfy "kinde," or sexual desire and accord with "reson," or intellectual power, not to be ruined by "lustes ignorance":

> The Philosophre upon this thing
> Writ and conseileth to a king,
> That he the surfet of luxure
> Schal tempre and reule of such mesure,
> Which be to *kinde* sufficant
> And ek to *reson* acordant,
> So that the lustes ignorance
> Be cause of no misgovernance,
> Thurgh which that he be overthrowe,
> As he that wol no *reson* knowe.
> For bot a mannes *wit* be swerved,
> Whan *kinde* is dueliche served,
> It oghte of *reson* to suffise;
> For if it falle him otherwise,
> He mai tho lustes sore drede. (7.4559-73)

Gower's view of moderation is well expressed.

15. Interesting is the story of Tobias and Sara (7.5307-5397), from which an eclectic solution is drawn. Sara is depicted as a beautiful

woman:

> Of bodi bothe and of visage
> Was non so fair of the lignage,
> To seche among hem alle, as sche. (7.5317-19)

Her former seven husbands, on their wedding night, had their necks wrung by Asmod, a fiend of hell, because they had intemperate sexual desire in consummating the marriage with her. Their asking "hire to wedde" (7.5323) was "more for likinge,/ To have his lust, than for weddinge" (7.5325-26).

By contrast, Tobias controlled his natural impulse by the archangel Raphael's advice. He succeeded in eschewing from death penalty to have kept moderation between reason and passion:

> For he his lust so goodly ladde,
> That bothe *lawe* and *kinde* is served,
> Wherof he hath himself preserved,
> That he fell noght in the sentence. (7.5362-65)

As referred to elsewhere, God established the laws towards not only "reson," but also "kinde," meaning "the natural instincts, desires." God bound beasts to the laws of nature only, but gave man both *kinde* and reason.

Tobias could keep "lustes" or natural impulse under the control of reason so as to both avoid lechery and have sexual appetite. "Reson" is equivalent in meaning to "word" and "langage," as in "The word to man hath yove alone" (7.1509) and "he can reson and langage" (6.1622). Diane Watt says that "Genius argues for the supremacy of reason, which should always control the will and lust".[22]

> For god the lawes hath assissed
> Als wel to *reson* as to *kinde*,
> Bot he the bestes wolde binde
> Only to *lawes of nature*,
> Bot to the mannes creature
> God yaf him *reson* forth withal,
> Wherof that he *nature* schal
> Upon the causes modefie,
> That he schal do no lecherie,
> And yit he schal hise lustes have. (7.5372-81)

Beasts, bound with the "lawes of nature" meaning "a consistent principle controlling the action of material things, law of nature, physical law," are permitted to act freely as nature or instinct directs, while man, endowed with reason, must "modifie" or regulate nature, which distinguishes man from beasts, as H.A. Klauser states.[23] Both man and beasts are controlled by the law of nature, but man alone has a responsibility of constraining nature and exercising reason.

16. Genius' advice is that it is proper for a man to love "be weie of kinde," which the *MED* takes to mean "in accordance with natural feelings or desires." "Gower occasionally uses 'kinde' to refer alternatively to natural appetite and reason," as Kurt Olsson notes:[24]

> It sit a man *be weie of kinde*
> To love, bot it is noght *kinde*
> A man for love his wit to lese. (7.4297-99)

Derek Pearsall remarks that "Like man in general, the lover must eschew the deadly sins, even lechery, for characteristic theme which Gower develops in the *Confessio* is of the control of blind passion through the exercise of reason, and of marriage as the true goal of 'fyn lovynge'."[25] "Kinde" (4298) means "proper, appropriate, fitting." "Wit" means "intellect, reason."

17. The king Eolus, god of the winds, had two children named Canace and Machaire, who always dwelled together. As they grew up, they began to have tender affection for each other and finally yielded to the law of nature or passion against "reson." This story is not the *exemplum* against incest, but that against her father's wrath:

> Into the youthe of lusti age,
> Whan *kinde* assaileth the corage
> With love and doth him forto bowe,
> That he no *reson* can allowe,
> Bot halt the *lawes of nature*. (3.153-57)

But the story of Canace and Machaire is concerned with incest. On the basis of Thomas Aquinas, Diane Watt says that "The inclusion of the personifications, Nature, kinde, and love, alongside Cupid contributes to our sense that the two lovers are subject to external forces beyond their control. In suggesting that incest can be driven by instinct, Genius follows Thomist definitions, which imply that although incest is to be condemned as a form of unchastity, it is not necessarily contrary to nature".[26]

As mentioned before, both of them did not commit incest, but were enchanted:

> And so it fell hem ate laste,
> That this Machaire with Canace
> Whan thei were in a prive place,
> Cupide bad hem ferst to kesse,
> And after sche which is Maistresse
> In kinde and techeth every lif
> Withoute lawe positif,
> Of which sche takth nomaner charge,
> Bot kepth hire lawes al at large,
> Nature, tok hem into lore
> And tawht hem so, that overmore
> Sche hath hem in such wise daunted,
> That thei were, as who seith, *enchaunted*. (3.166-78)

"Because of youth and ignorance, law has not yet been promulgated through their reason. From the outset, Gower makes this dichotomy between nature and reason quite pointed," as Klauser put it.[27]

A living being acts according to the law of nature. What the goddess Nature set "in hir lawe" (3.55) cannot be canceled by human power. If a man acts contrary to the law, he is sure to incur "gret vengance" (3.359), or Heaven's retribution.

The *MED* defines nature as "Nature as governed by law; natural law as the norm of human experience and the basis of probability; as an ineluctable force; as a quasi-personified creditor to whom man is indebted":

> What *nature* hath set in hir lawe
> Ther mai no mannes miht withdrawe,
> And who that worcheth therayein,
> Fulofte time it hath be sein,
> Ther hath befalle gret vengance,
> Wherof I finde a remembrance. (3.355-60)

Machaire illicitly fell in love with Canace thus:

> Whan *kinde* assaileth the corage
> With *love* and doth him forto bowe,
> That he no *reson* can allowe,
> Bot halt *the lawes of nature*. (3.154-57)

"Kinde" means "natural instincts or desires." Here "kinde" takes away reason by assailing "the corage With love," which usually occurs in cooperation with love, which is blind (3.159). Love is portrayed as follows:

> For *love is of a wonder kinde,*
> *And hath hise wittes ofte blinde,*
> *That thei fro mannes reson falle;*

> *Bot whan that it is so befalle*
> *That will schal the corage lede,*
> *In loves cause it is to drede.* (3.1323-28).

Genius underlines and emphasizes the power of will in love and explicitly suggests the necessity of reason to control will or passion. After Canace had committed an illicit love, she conceived a child. It is the natural desires that are deeply embedded in his heart. Nature is directly opposed to the *lex positiva*.

18. "Kinde" is used to indicate birth. In the story of Constance, the word *kinde* occurs in the birth of the prince, one of the three typical happenings. Constance was safely delivered of a son at the date he was due:

> The time *set of kinde* is come,
> This lady hath hire chambre nome,
> And of a Sone bore full,
> Wherof that sche was joiefull,
> Sche was delivered sauf and sone. (2.931-35)

"The time set of kinde" means "the expected date of confinement."

19. "Kinde" governs not only birth and growth, but also death. "Ther was of *kinde* bot a lite,/ That thei ne semen fulli dede" (1.2046-47), which means "they have but a few days to live."

The king of Hungary had a proud brother. When the trumpet of death was blown before the door, it was to be destined that the husband could not eschew from death. One day, the trumpet was blown in front of his brother's door, so that all the family were panic-stricken. They hurried naked to the king to plead for his life. The king told about the difference between "deth, which stant under the lawe/ Of man" (1.2223-24) and "deth../ Which god hath set be lawe of kinde" (1.2230-31) and so emphasized humility and nature. Furthermore, he went on to say that the sentence of death passed by men can be withdrawn, but the death set by God cannot be escaped. The man's life span is set "be lawe of kinde," "so schal deie" (1.2235). The king himself had a sign of his own death through the image of two aged pilgrims and said to his haughty brother:

>For that thou seist thou art in doute
>Of deth, which stant under the lawe
>Of man, and man it mai withdrawe,
>So that it mai par chance faile.
>Now schalt thou noght forthi mervaile
>That I doun fro my Charr alihte,
>Whanne I behield tofore my sihte
>In hem that were of so gret age
>*Min oghne deth* thurgh here ymage,
>Which god hath set *be lawe of kynde*,
>Wherof I mai no bote finde: (1.2222-32)

Probably Gower also may have brought his death to mind through his portraiture. In this way, the king made lucid the contrast between man's laws and God's "kinde."

"Kinde" governs the natural world emphatically enumerated such as man and bird and beast and flower and grass and root and tree and every thing, all of which shall starve (in its original sense of 'to die') "be weie of kynde":

> For every man and bridd and beste,
> And flour and gras and rote and rinde,
> And every thing *be weie of kynde*
> Schal sterve, and Erthe it schal become;
> As it was out of Erthe nome,
> It schal to therthe torne ayein. (1.3260-65)

It is the doom of all creatures that they shall return to the earth after death. No birth without death, as the proverb says.

It is division that makes the world fall. Similarly man must die "naturally," since the elements in his constitution ("complexioun") is made on division of cold, hot, moist, and dry. The four complexions or humours are blood, phleigm, cholar, and melancholy:

> Division aboven alle
> Is thing which makth the world to falle,
> And evere hath do sith it began.
> It may ferst proeve upon a man;
> The which, for his complexioun
> Is mad upon divisioun
> Of cold, of hot, of moist, of drye,
> He mot *be verray kynde dye*. (Prol. 971-78)

123

"Be verray kynde" means "by nature, naturally."

The word *kinde* (3.1572) occurs in the king Allee's death, one of the three typical happenings. Moreover, "kinde" appears in the place where Constance's father died a "deth of kinde," which means "he lived out a natural life," embraced in her arms:

> And after that the bokes sein,
> She was noght there bot a throwe,
> Whan *deth of kinde* hath overthrowe
> Hir worthi fader, which men seide
> That he between hire armes deide. (2.1586-90)

Alchemists makes three philosophers' stones "be weie of kinde" (4.2532) to transform base metals like lead and tin, into precious metals like gold and silver. One of the stones called *lapis vegetabilis* has the virtue of medicines which heal the sick and protect persons from illness until a natural death comes:

> *[lapis vegetabilis]..*
> Of which the propre vertu is
> To mannes hele forto serve,
> As forto kepe and to preserve
> The bodi fro siknesses alle,
> Til *deth of kinde* upon him falle. (4.2536-40)

"Deth of kinde," personified here, means "the god of natural death."

A man endowed with "reson" should not die like beasts until he dies naturally:

> For every lif which *reson* can
> Oghth wel to knowe that a man
> Ne scholde thurgh no tirannie
> Lich to these othre bestes die,
> Til *kinde* wolde for him sende.
> I not hou he it mihte amende,
> Which takth awei for everemore
> The lif that he mai noght restore. (3.2473-80)

Allegorically speaking, "kinde," which is personified or deified as the god of death, means "a natural death."

The poem, called *Last Poems*, begins with "Quiquid homo scribat" consisting of the six lines, in which Gower describes that he became "cecus" or lost his sight. The first line begins with "finem natura ministrant":

> Quicquid homo scribat, *finem natura ministrat,*
> Que velut vmbra fugit, nec fugiendo redit;
> Illa michi finem posuit, quo scribere quicquam
> Vlterius nequio, *sum* quia *cecus ego.*
> Posse meum transit, quamuis michi velle remansit;
> Amplius vt scribat hoc michi posse neqat. (1-6)

20. In winter, which is stormy "be weie of kinde" or naturally, first winds blow and then it rains with the watergates open. It is natural force only, not human power that can give rise to these phenomena:

> For it was wynter time tho,
> And wynter, as *be weie of kinde*
> Which stormy is, as men it finde,
> Ferst makth the wyndes forto blowe,
> And after that withinne a throwe
> He reyneth and the watergates
> Undoth; (3.684-90)

Thus meteorological phenomena are applied figuratively to the familiar story of Xanthippe, Socrates' wife.

According to the Greek myths, Narcissus took his own pretty figure reflected in the fountain for a nymph, with which he fell in love and breathed his last. Even in the middle of winter, daffodils unusually began to come from within his sepulcher, which is "contraire to kynde":

> For in the wynter freysshe and faire
> The floures ben, which is *contraire*
> *To kynde*, and so was the folie
> Which fell of his Surquiderie. (1.2355-58)

It is traditionally common in a literary mileu that flowers, with the exception of specific kind, bloom in spring and wither in winter. Blooming in winter seems to be out of season. Thus Gower makes prominent the likeness between the self-love of Narcissus and the untimely blooming of flowers.

Sardana Pallas, king of Assyria, went insane with love, so that he became awfully womanish and effeminate. He shut himself in the room "as if a fish would live on the land," and took pleasure in working at women's will, which is "ayein kinde":

> [Sardana Pallus]..
> ..wax so ferforth womannyssh,
> That *ayein kinde*, as if a fissh
> Abide wolde upon the lond,
> In wommen such a lust he fond,
> That he duelte evere in chambre stille,
> And only wroghte after the will
> Of wommen, so as he was bede. (7.4321-27)

21. Incest, which is immoral, is one of the Seven Deadly Sins. Amon lay with his sister Tamaru unnaturally, so that he was killed by Absalom, his brother. The *MED* takes the noun *thunkinde* (222) to mean "one who commits incest," which is recorded as the first instance:

> Amon his Soster *ayein kinde*,
> Which hihte Thamar, he forlay;
> Bot he that lust an other day
> Aboghte, whan that Absolon
> His oghne brother therupon,
> Of that he hadde his Soster schent,
> Tok of that Senne vengement
> And slowh him with his oghne hond:
> And thus *thunkinde unkinde* fond. (8.214-22)

127

"Unkinde" means "contrary to the natural moral law." "In Absolom's case," H.A. Klauser remarks, "the Confessor shows some sympathy, but nevertheless points out that it is unnatural to kill your brother under any circumstances."[28]

"Unkinde" is frequently used to illustrate homicide. For example, Chrytemnestra, a "cruel beste unkinde," killed her husband Agamemnon in conspiracy with her lover Aigist. The son Orestes abused her in the presence of others and took vengeance on her for his father's murder:

> 'O cruel beste *unkinde*,
>   How mihtest thou thin herte finde,
>   For eny lust of loves drawhte,
>   That thou acordest to the slawhte
>   Of him which was thin oghne lord? (3.2055-59)

The *MED* takes "unkinde" here to mean "lacking natural affection for a spouse." It is "unkinde" to kill a spouse.

At the head of a line, the adverbs *unkindely* and *unkindeliche* are placed to emphasize her immoral acts. Orestes slayed his mother. "The Confessor does not condemn him," H.A. Klauser writes, "but yet retains an awareness that it is equally unnatural for a son to kill his mother as it was for the mother to kill her husband. Orestes himself acknowledges the grim irony, saying to his mother":[29]

> *Unkindely* for thou hast wroght,
>   *Unkindeliche* it schal be boght, (3.2065-66)

The *MED* takes the former to mean "in violation of the marriage bond" and the latter to mean "in violation of the natural obligation of children to parents." James Simpson provides a similar opinion concerning this story: "In this tale, the structure of events forces the reader to recognize the inadequacy of the 'lawe of kynde' alone, in either politics or love. The speech of Orestes to Clytemnestra forces the limitations of the law of 'kynde'; is one 'unkynde' act justly dealt with by another?"[30]

22. The story of Ulysses and Telegonus is not fit for the theme of Gluttony, but shows its close relationship to Gower's intention in terms of "kinde" and "kindeliche" love.

If a man attempts to practise sorcery and witchcraft in good faith, he can do them "be weie of kinde":

> For these craftes, as I finde,
> A man mai do *be weie of kinde,*
> Be so it be *to good entente.* (6.1303-5)

When witchcraft is practised, the manner of both "be weie of kinde" and "to good entente" are a necessary condition, because witchcraft is apt to fall into an act of cheating others. H.A. Klauser remarks that "It is important to keep this qualification in mind when reading of Ulysses' fate."[31]

Excepting the virtue of "kindeschipe," Ulysses was well acquainted with every field of learning such as rhetoric, astronomy, philosophy, medicine, surgery, and magic. Sailing home from Troy, he, with his men, was driven by a storm to the shore of

Sicily, where he met the two goddess queens Calypso and Cerce, who knew how to practise supernatural craft:

> Ther myhte hem nothing desobeie,
> Such craft thei hadde *above kinde*. (6.1452-53)

The phrase *above kinde* means "of transcending natural physical order of things."

They attempted to woo him through their magic, but failed. They succeeded, however, in transforming all the men of his "navie" (6.1445) into owls as well as beasts like bears, tigers, and apes, with the exception of Ulysses, because their magic had not in the least effect on him, while he made them "wilde" (6.1462) or lusty and fled away by ship:

> Circes *toswolle* bothe sides
> He lefte. (6.1467-68)

Cerce was great with child. Eventually she begot a son named Telegonus.

Through sorcery, he satisfied his lust. Through sorcery, his grief began. Through sorcery, he got his love. Through sorcery, he lost his life. Note the repetition of "Sorcerie" (6.1768, 1773) and "Through Sorcerie" (6.1769, 1670, 1671, 1672). The son who committed a great crime was born through sorcery. Thus,

> Thing which was *ayein kynde* wroght
> *Unkindeliche* it was aboght;

> The child his oghne fader slowh,
> That was *unkindeschipe* ynogh. (6.1775-78)

"Unkindeliche" implies "with unnatural disregard for a parent." "Unkindeschipe" means "an unfilial or undutiful act." Gower's judgment is that it is unfilial or contrary to humanity to slay a father.

The *MED* takes "unkinde" to mean "untrue to a lover," referring to "also, as noun: a cruel deceiver":

> 'O thou *unkinde*,
> Hier schalt thou thurgh thi Slowthe finde,
> If that thee list to come and se
> A ladi ded for love of thee,
> So as I schal myselve spille. (4.849-53)

Other examples are (5.535) and (5.5479).

"Unkinde" means "lacking in charity, ungenerous, stingy":

> And for he wolde noght ben holde
> *Unkinde*, he tok his cause on honde,
> And as it were of goddes sonde,
> He yaf him good ynouh to spende
> For evere into his lives ende. (7.2102-6)

"Kinde" means "man's innate or instinctive moral feeling":

> For yet was nevere such covine,

>That couthe ordeine a medicine
>To thing which god in *lawe of kinde*
>Hath set, for ther may noman finde
>The rihte salve of such a Sor. (1.29-33)

The *MED* takes "lawe of kinde," listed as the first recorded example, to mean "natural moral law."

23. The cruel king Lichaon ("a wolf" in Greek) had, in a literal sense, a wolfish character, who would kill his customers whose flesh he made others devour. He violated "kinde" in slaying his guests. It is worthwhile to note that "kinde," as in "ayein the lawe of kinde," listed as the first recorded example in the *MED*, implies "against the moral law peculiar to man having a rational soul." Moral law is considered to be implanted by God in man's natural reason:

>Of Lichaon also I finde
>Hou he *ayein the lawe of kinde*
>Hise hostes slouh, and into mete
>He made her bodies to ben ete
>With othre men withinne his hous. (7.3355-59)

His acts are against the natural moral law. At last Jupiter transformed Lichaon literally into a wolf. The *OED* takes "nature" to mean "the inherent and innate disposition" of a wolf:

>A wolf he was thanne openly,
>The whos *nature* prively

He hadde in his condicion. (7.3367-69)

The distortion of natural word order is utilized clearly to emphasize "A wolf," as in "A wolf he was" (7.3367).

24. The same idea is found in the story of Tereus and Procne. False Tereus did cruel acts to Philomela, sister of his wife Procne. Gower portrays Tereus as "The most untrewe and most *unkinde/ That evere in ladi armes lay*" (5.5836-37). Philomela angrily chopped the son into small pieces, whom the husband dearly loved, out of which she mades stew, adding spices and offered it to Tereus. As he was "unkinde," he ate it "ayein kinde." To make Tereus realize how it happened, Philomela presented on the table the son's head pressed between two dishes:

> That he ne wiste hou that it stod,
> Bot thus his oughne fleissh and blod
> Himself devoureth *ayein kinde*,
> As he that was tofore *unkinde*.
> And thanne, er that he were arise,
> For that he scholde ben agrise,
> To schewen him the child was ded,
> This Philomene tok the hed
> Betwen tuo disshes, and al wrothe
> Tho comen forth the Sostres bothe,
> And setten it upon the bord. (5.5903-13)

Finally the trio of Philomela, Procne, and Tereus were transformed into birds, such as nightingale, swallow, and lapwing respectively.

25. Genius tells about the virtue of "Misericorde," or pity. God made natural and moral law to which man is bound and told him proverbially: Do to others as you would they should do to you. This proverb is based on Luke 6:31:

> And ek he tok a remembrance
> How he that made *lawe of kinde*
> Wolde every man to *lawe* binde,
> And bad a man, such as he wolde
> Toward himself, riht such he scholde
> Toward an other don also. (2.3274-79)

"Lawe of kinde," i.e. Natural Law, used in a good sense, binds man's reason to pity. Later Genius extends the association of love, pity and compassion with the "lawe of kinde" to war.[32]

The story of the worthy knights is told by the comparison of a virtue of mercy to a strange bird:

> For every *lawe* and every *kinde*
> The mannes wit to merci binde;
> And namely the worthi knihtes,
> Whan that thei stonden most uprihtes
> And ben most mihti forto grieve,
> Thei scholden thanne most relieve
> Him whom thei mihten overthrowe. (3.2631-37)

It is remarkable here that Gower puts a special emphasis on mercy towards the opposite party in time of war. A worthy knight, for example, will show mercy or pity on the enemies with whom he is fighting. Positive law is artificially made, while pity or mercy is natural and innate.

Gower declares that all the animals and plants on earth were made "newe ayein" after the Flood. Flower, fruit, grass, grain, beast, bird, and mankind, all of which had been ungrateful to God, were "renewed":

> After the flod, fro which Noë
> Was sauf, the world in his degre
> Was mad, as who seith, newe ayein,
> Of flour, of fruit, of gras, of grein,
> Of beste, of bridd and of mankinde,
> Which evere hath be to god *unkinde*. (5.1605-10)

The word *unkinde* means "lacking in natural gratitude or ungrateful."

26. Philip, king of Macedonia, had the two sons: Demetrius and Perseus. A younger brother Perseus basely slandered Demetrius to his father with the bad intention of entrapping him. He said "With false wordes" (2.1649):

> Mi diere fader, I am holde
> *Be weie of kinde*, as *resoun* wolde,
> That I fro yow schal nothing hide,

> Which mihte torne in eny side
> Of youre astat into grevance. (2.1653-57)

"Be weie of kinde" means "the natural obligation of children to parents." "As reson wolde" means "according to common sense."

As seen hitherto, the ME. value-words *love, Fortune, nature, kinde, lawe,* and *reson,* are closely related and mutually entangled in sense. It is difficult to make clear the mutual relation among them. Love is blind. Love changes reason into the law of kind, which deprives man of reason and makes a man blind. God gave "kinde" or instinct to beasts, while He gave both "kinde" and reason to man. Reason in this case means words or intellectual power. God gave words to man. Man must control sexual desire by virtue of words and live a reasonable life. Most of the moral judgment of good or evil in the stories are made by the terms *kinde* and *unkinde.*

Notes

1 Pickles, J.D., and J.L. Dawson (eds.), *A Concordance to John Gower's Confessio Amantis* (D.S. Brewer, 1990). Some common phrases are listed on the basis of *A Concordance* as below.
be weie of kinde (34) (1.3262, 2.1654, 2.3138, 2.3211, 3.685, 3.2582, 4.2508, 4.2532, 4.2873, 5.252, 5.282, 5.859, 5.4919, 5.6422, 6.1304, 7.252, 7.460, 7.598, 7.787, 7.796, 7.1358, 7.1428, 7.1484, 7.1667, 7.1869, 7.4217, 7.4297, 7.4385), lawe of kinde (1.31, 1.2231, 2.3275, 7.233-4, 7.3356, 8.3146), be kinde (P.978, 1.1506, 4.932, 6.1149), ayein kinde (5.4924, 5.5905, 6.1156, 6.1775, 7.2215, 7.4322, 8.214, 8.2007, 8.2017, cf.2.3398, 7.3356), after kinde (3.353, 3.390, 4.2255, 5.825, cf.7.441), above kinde (4.438, 6.1453), out of kinde (4.1936, 5.6004, 7.5220), be weie of nature (5.4919, 8.1089), be nature (2.3053), ayein Nature (8.2339), after the natures (7.872), after the natures of his age (5.2649), after the lawe of nature (4.3200, 5.4930, 7.1049), loves kinde (1.309,

"Kinde" and Related Terms in John Gower's *Confessio Amantis*

1.2781, 5.2829, 5.4796, 5.5423, 7.5426, 8.2028, 8.2371, cf.4.1615), mones kinde (7.1321), mannes kind (3.1784, 4.1088, 5.186, 5.6372, 7.442, 7.3489, 7.4743), sharmebudes kinde (2.413), worldes kinde (6.1265), houndes kinde (2.84, 2.1795), briddes kinde (4.3119, 5.5939), kinde of man (4.2934, 5.2, 7.402, cf. 2.3398), kinde of briddes (1.2826), kinde of foules (5.1206), kinde of bestes (1.2828), deth of kinde (2.2.1588, 4.2540), a wonder kinde (1.484, 3.2600, 6.284), bodiliche kinde (2.3344), wommanisshe kinde (5.6199), the creatour of alle kinde (7.6199), the god of kinde (8.2239), take kinde (7.421, 7.1331, 7.1341, 7.1381, 7.1404), of kinde (2.931, 4.5, 5.2829, 7.912, 7.1133, 7.1373, 7.1420, 7.1154, 7.1195, 7.1219, 8.994, 8.2020, 8.2228), of...kinde (1.773, 1.1026, 1.1360, 3.1366, 4.3432, 7.1292, 7.2469), of his oghne kinde (5.323, 7.732), of the same kinde (5.6494, 7.340), lawes of nature (3.157, 4.3200, 7.5375), nature of (4.321, 6.531, 6.812, 7.25), of...nature (4.2250), The hihe makere of nature(s (2.916, 7.1508), god of nature (5.1041).

2 *The Complete Works of John Gower* 4 vols., vol.1 (The French Works, 1899), vols.2,3 (The English Works, 1901), vol.4 (The Latin Works,1902), ed. by G,C, Macaulay (Oxford: at the Clarendon Press; Scholarly Press, Republ. 1968). All quotations from John Gower are from *The Complete Works*.

3 Peck, R.A. (ed.), *Confessio Amantis* (New York, 1968), p.xv.

4 Coffman, "George R., "Jon Gower in his Most Significant Role": *Elizabethan Studies and Other Essays in Honor of George F. Reynolds* (Colorado, 1945), p. 219.

5 Economou, G.D., *The Goddes Natura in Medieval Literature* (Cambridge, Mass.: Harvard University Press, 1972), p. 2.

6 Wilson, W.B., *A Translation of John Gower's* Mirour de l'Omme, Pt. 1 (Univ. Microfilms, 1970).

7 Olsson, Kurt, "Natural Law and John Gower's Confessio *Amantis,*" *Medievalia et Humanistica: Studies in Medieval and Renaissance Culture*, New Series, 11 (1982), pp.187-188.

8 Fox, George G., *The Medieval Sciences in the Works of John Gower*, (Princeton, 1931), p.6.

9 Brewer, D.S. (ed.), *The Parlement of Foulys*, pp.26-30.

10 *The Riverside Chaucer*, ed. by Larry D. Benson, 3rd Ed. (Boston: Houghton Mifflin).

11 Olsson, Kurt, *op.cit.*, pp.187-188.

12 Echard, Siân and Claire Fanger (tr.), *The Latin Verses in the Confessio Amantis: An Annotated Translation* (East Lansing: Colleague Press, 1991), pp.41-42

13 Fox, *op.cit.*, p.6.

14 Stockton, Eric W., *The Major Latin Works of John Gower: The Voice of*

one Crying and the Tripartite Chronicle (Seattle: University of Washington Press, 1962), p.114.
15   J.A.W. Bennett, *Selections from John Gower* (Oxford, 1968), p.143.
16   Bennett, *op.cit.*, p.x.
17   White, Hugh, "Nature and the Good in Gower's *Confessio Amantis*": *John Gower: Recent Readings*, ed. by R.F. Yeager (Kalamazoo, Michigan: Western Michigan University, 1989), p.6.
18   White, *op. cit.*, p.7.
19   Klauser, H.A., *The Concept of* "kynde": *John Gower's* Confessio Amantis (Univ. Microfilms, Ann Arbor, Michigan, 1972), p.53.
20   Burrow, John, "Gower's Poetic Styles": *A Companion to Gower*, ed. by Siân Echard (D.S. Brewer, 2004), p.246.
21   Bennett, *op.cit.*, p.ix
22   Watt, Diane, "Gender and Sexuality in *Confessio Amantis*": *A Companion to Gower*, ed. by Siân Echard (D.S. Brewer, 2004), p.202.
23   Klauser, *op.cit.*, p.53.
24   Olsson, *op.cit.*, p.194.
25   Pearsall, Derek, *Gower and Lydgate* (London, 1969), p.13.
26   Watt, *op.cit.*, p.200.
27   Klauser, *op.cit.*, p.151.
28   Klauser, *op.cit.*, p.35.
29   Klauser, *op.cit.*, p.35.
30   Simpson, James, *Sciences and the Self in Medieval Poetry: Alan of Lille's Anticlaudianus & John Gower's* Confessio Amantis (Cambridge University Press, 1995), p.190.
31   Klauser, *op.cit.*, p.159.
32   Olsson, *op.cit.*, pp.187-188.

Contributors

Masahiko Agari, Professor Emeritus, Saga University

Kazuko Matsuura, Part-time Lecturer, Okayama University of Science

Motoko Sando, Part-time Lecturer, Wakayama University

Saoko Tomita, Lecturer, Faculty of Humanities, Fukuoka University

Koichi Totani, Part-time Lecturer, Chukyo University

Masahiko Kanno, Professor Emeritus, Aichi University of Education